FLYNN

"is one of the smartest, gentlest, most sarcastic cops you will ever meet!"
The New York Times

GREGORY McDONALD

"is the toughest, leanest horse to hit the literary racetrack since James M. Cain, and it's sheer pleasure to watch him make his run."
Pete Hamill

THE BUCK PASSES FLYNN
BY
GREGORY MCDONALD

THE BUCK PASSES FLYNN

GREGORY McDONALD

BALLANTINE BOOKS • NEW YORK

Library of Congress Catalog Card Number: 81-66358

ISBN 0-345-31610-X

Manufactured in the United States of America

First Edition: December 1981
Third Printing: September 1983

Verse on p. 53 from *The Lake of Innisfree*, William Butler
Yeats, 1865–1939

1

From across the men's room Flynn aimed his gun at the President of the United States.

The President had said, "I don't need you guys to help me do what I'm about to do," and closed the door on the crowd of Secret Service agents and other aides in the hotel corridor. He nodded to the agent stationed in the men's room, who smiled and nodded back and left. Believing himself alone, taking a small plastic vial of eyedrops from his pocket, the President stepped to a washbasin. It was while he was using the mirror, applying the eyedrops, that he saw Flynn appear through the wall behind him.

"Oh, Lord." The President dropped the plastic vial into the washbasin. He turned around. "I'm dead."

"That you are," agreed Flynn. "Deader than a campaign promise."

Through a peephole, Flynn had watched the President enter the men's room. As soon as the President busied himself at the washbasin, Flynn slid aside the panel he had built into the false wall and stepped out, gun in hand.

The President glanced at the door to the corridor. "What if I yell?"

"It will come out a whistle," Flynn assured him, raising his aim, "through the wee hole in your throat."

The President nodded at the front of Flynn's handgun. "That's a silencer."

"It is," confirmed Flynn. "It permits me to empty the gun into you without threat of interference."

The President was trying to look around Flynn, at the wall behind him, a section of which was missing. "How did you do it? How did you get in here?"

"I didn't get in here. I was in here."

"You couldn't have been. There was a Secret Service agent in here."

"A man with the unfortunate habit of suckin' his teeth when he's nervous. I was here before him."

"You couldn't have been here while they were checking the room. They would have put you out."

"I was here," said Flynn, "watching them. They checked the room twice, they did. They even opened the cabinet door and flushed the toilet. And, in fact, they did ask an old man to leave, an hour ago, sayin' they were securin' the room. He'd been here a dreadful long time. I think he was tryin' to pass a stone. Sure, they could have given him another ten minutes." Flynn continued in his soft, rapid lilt. "The Secret Service made the same presumption I did, you see, that most likely you'd use the bathroom nearest the speaker's platform here at the Waldorf-Astoria, to straighten your tie, clear your eyes, pat your hair, practice your smile in the mirror, whatever, before being introduced to . . . who is it? Who's waiting to hear you speak?"

"The Brotherhood of Christians and Jews."

"Ach," said Flynn, "a noble group. Won't they be surprised to hear you've been shot right in the middle of their salad? They'll know the right prayers to say over you, that group will."

"I want to know how—"

"Are you really interested? Or are you merely stallin' for time, Mister President, thinkin' that one of your Secret Service agents—good lads that they are—might get curious and come through that door, lookin' to see how things came out?"

"You're standing there with a gun on me. If one does come through that door, you're deader than—than—"

"Yesterday's joy?"

"Yesterday's joy."

"Deader than last year's pain?"

"You mean to torture me with your humor—"

"I mean to shoot you. The locked-door mystery, Mister President. Do you read mysteries?"

The President blushed. "I don't read anything else —voluntarily."

"Then you know all about the locked-door mystery. You might consider this room locked, in that it has been searched, everyone's been put out of it—except you, the victim—there is no window, there is no way in, except through that door, which has rows of guards outside it. And yet here you are, about to be found shot."

"How did you get in?"

"You keep asking that. I didn't get in. I was in. False wall." Flynn kicked the wall behind him with his heel. "See how the panels fit together?"

The President nodded.

"I finished putting it up yesterday noon. In my Johnny Strong overalls and Black and Decker cap. The hotel staff was very helpful to me. They kept out of my way and let me do my work. Of course people always cooperate with people doin' work they might be asked to do themselves."

"You've been behind the wall—the false wall—all night?"

"With thermoses of tea, a dozen sandwiches, and, of course, access to a perfectly fine men's room. There have been times I've had it worse." Flynn waved his

3

gun impatiently. "If you don't mind, Mister President, it's been nice chattin' with you and all that, but let's get on with it. Any last words for the library wall?"

"You're not going to—"

"I am. Would you mind opening your suit jacket a wee bit, so I won't miss the heart?"

"People are waiting for me to give a speech—"

"Aren't they always, though?"

"The Brotherhood of Christians and Jews—"

"Open your jacket, please, Mister President. You don't want to spoil my aim, do you?"

The President flapped open his suit jacket.

Flynn shot the President of the United States in the heart.

The President said, "Ouch."

"Stings a little?"

The President looked down at himself. "Thank God," he said. "The suitcoat will cover it."

"That's what I was thinkin'," said Flynn. "You about to make a speech and all."

"What is it?" The President was still looking at the goo on his chest.

"Ketchup and soy sauce. I've been ordered to provide evidence you've been assassinated," Flynn said, "without actually doin' the deed, that is."

"You were given a week to assassinate me." The President was breathing a little heavily. "And you did it within three days."

"The point is proven?"

"You and that little guy—"

"N.N. Zero."

"Yeah—said you could break through security within any given week."

"Three days, Mister President."

"And knowing you were trying, security around me was tripled this week. What did the Secret Service do wrong?"

"They failed to see something that wasn't there." Flynn placed his handgun on the sandwich wrappers behind the false wall. "I'm sure there are bathrooms without windows, but they're rare. Any bathroom without either a window or an air-conditioning system, I wouldn't want to use. Do you see either a window or an air-conditioning system in this bathroom, Mister President?"

The President's eyes surveyed the room quickly. "No."

"Yet on the outside of this building, there is a window for this room. Therefore, in this room, there had to be a false wall." Flynn smiled at the President. "Behind that false wall lurked an assassin. And in you sauntered, believin' you were as alone as if you'd lost the New Hampshire Primary."

The President buttoned his coat. "You've proven your point."

"Have we indeed?" Flynn answered easily. "The Secret Service agents, good lads that they are, Mister President, are prone to obey your wishes, because you're the President of the United States. The agent you just sent out of this room with a nod of your head should never have left." Without having washed his hands, Flynn dried them on a towel. "You have no right to endanger yourself, Mister President. Every time you think everything's been thought of, think again." Flynn dropped the towel into a bucket. "Excuse me for not stayin' for lunch. I'm full of sandwiches and tea."

Just as Flynn reached the men's room door, the President said his name.

"Yes, Mister President?"

"I have a message for you," the President said laconically. "Call your office."

"Thank you, Mister President."

"The little guy called this morning. N.N. Zero. Asked me to give you the message. Said I'd be seeing you before he would. Thought he was kidding."

"That particular little guy," said Flynn, "never kids."

5

*   *   *

Flynn came through the men's room door showing everyone in the corridor his most beguiling smile.

The Secret Service agents, good lads that they are, gasped and reached for their guns.

"Is there another men's room nearby?" Flynn asked innocently. "This one's occupied."

2

"N.N. 13," Flynn said into the telephone.

In the lobby of the Hotel Waldorf-Astoria, Flynn had dialed the Pittsburgh number and given the operator his credit-card number.

The man who answered drawled, "Are you free?"

"Yes. I'm in New York."

"One moment, please."

In the lobby Flynn watched a man and a woman greet each other. He guessed her clothes cost thousands of dollars. The man's suit and shoes, too, looked as if they cost plenty. Nearby stood a little girl. Dressing her had probably cost hundreds of dollars. Scanning everyone in the lobby, Flynn wondered what the total value of their clothes was. Probably more dollars than it took to dress the entire Continental Army.

"13?"

"Yes," Flynn answered.

"Zero. 1600. Lions' cage, the zoo."

"Rightio," said Flynn. "Rightio."

3

Down the path the little man stood near the lions' cage. Three tall men were standing around him.

Flynn knew N.N. Zero—John Roy Priddy—liked places where there were apt to be other small human beings—playgrounds, circuses, zoos. N.N. Zero was three feet ten inches high.

Flynn had bought two bags of peanuts.

"Hello, Frank." N.N. Zero reached up to shake hands.

"Hello, sir." Flynn did not stoop. From all the years working with N.N. Zero, Flynn knew well it was no kindness to stoop to him. It was a cruelty.

N.N. Zero was a little person, and he spoke softly.

Flynn maintained his posture and was grateful for his acute hearing.

N.N. Zero looked absently around at the three men with him.

They absented themselves.

There was calliope music, *Octopus's Garden.*

"How's Elsbeth?" N.N. Zero asked.

"Fine."

"Todd?"

"Fine."

"Randy?"

"Fine."

Flynn handed N.N. Zero a bag of peanuts.

N.N. Zero handed Flynn a fifty-dollar bill.

Flynn glanced at it and put it in his pocket.

"Jenny?"

"Fine."

"Winny?"

"Fine."

"Jeff?"

"Fine."

N.N. Zero was always solicitous about Flynn's wife and children, asking for them each in order. He actually knew each of their characteristics as well, even to twelve-year-old Jenny not yet knowing she was gorgeous and nine-year-old Winny not yet knowing his compulsion to be a wit.

"Well, Frank. Did you knock off the President?"

"Before lunch."

"Was he appreciative?"

"He seemed mostly appreciative I didn't mess up his shirt. He had to give a speech."

"Running a private organization like N.N., Frank, we'll always need funds, and we'll always need access to the President of the United States. And as long as there is a K., there's a need for N.N. Yet no President, once he's told about us, believes in us much. We have to prove ourselves to every President, in some personal way. . . ."

N.N. Zero opened his bag and threw a peanut into the lions' cage.

At the back of the cage lay a lion and a lioness. They were flea-bitten and fat but pretty together.

N.N. Zero asked, "Are you ready for an odd story, Frank?"

"The Irish love a story," said Francis Xavier Flynn, N.N. 13. "Don't we just?"

"Trouble is," said N.N. Zero, "we don't know the

beginning of this story. Nor do we know the end of it. Maybe we're putting three things together that don't belong together. I don't know. Odd things have happened at three different places on the map. And I think they may have something in common. And even if they do, I'm not sure what it is, or what to make of it. The most recent event—if these are events—concerns us."

Flynn shelled a peanut and tossed it into the lions' cage.

Neither lion moved.

"About twelve weeks ago," N.N. Zero said, "there were one thousand eight hundred and fifty-six people, men, women, and children, living in the town of Ada, Texas. Today, as far as we know, there are two.

"One day the minister in that town, a Reverend Sandy Fraiman, called the office of the Federal Bureau of Investigation in Austin, and said that everyone in the town, except himself and his wife, had disappeared."

"Disappeared?" Flynn rubbed his ear. "This isn't a flying-saucer story, is it? I don't like flying-saucer stories. They upset my equilibrium."

"Everyone had left town except the minister and his wife."

" 'Left town.' Of their own volition, I take it. Tell me, sir. Do you think the man's sermons had been runnin' overlong? Were the people fleein' them, do you think?"

"The minister watched them leave. He called the F.B.I. on a Thursday. He said people had begun to leave town on the previous Saturday. More than half the town had left by Sunday night. The rest were gone by Wednesday. They simply packed up their cars and pickup trucks with personal belongings, and left. The minister stopped some of them and asked where they were going. Some said Dallas. Some said Oklahoma. Some said Las Vegas. Some said California."

"And none said the Promised Land? No wonder the minister was upset."

"The F.B.I. agent drove to Ada next day. He confirmed there appeared to be no one in town except the minister and his wife. He reported the minister appeared 'shaky.' "

"No wonder. He was the shepherd whose flock had escaped up the glen, waggin' their tails behind 'em."

"Get this, Flynn. After some questioning, the minister told the agent that on the previous Saturday morning he had found two large manila envelopes on his front porch, one with his name on it, one with his wife's name on it. In each envelope was one hundred thousand dollars in cash. Mostly fifty-dollar bills, some one hundreds, some twenties."

"Manna from Heaven."

"Exactly. The minister was delighted. He believes it's a gift to the church. It's a poor town, and apparently the church is in great disrepair. The F.B.I. agent filed his report, of course."

"Of course."

"The next week."

"Of course."

"A copy came to us in the pouch. A week after that."

Flynn tossed some peanuts he had shelled into the lions' cage.

"This made us mildly curious," N.N. Zero continued, "to see if any such similar incident had happened to any other small town in the United States. We discovered that in a small town in New England, the ministers left, and the townspeople stayed. East Frampton, Massachusetts—"

"I know the old place. Took my kids there summer before last. We ate at a—"

"A small island community, utterly dependent upon the tourist trade and a little fishing. Nothing more to worry about, if you'd believe it, than squashing rumors a shark with a yen for human flesh basted in suntan oil is prowling their waters."

"Not a refined taste, I think."

"The captain of the ferryboat, who lives on the mainland, mentioned to a fellow member of Kiwanis, who is a policeman in New Bedford, who told his chief, who mentioned it to the local F.B.I. agent—"

"Not a direct source comin' straight at us," commented Flynn.

"—that suddenly every trip he took his ferry was loaded with expensive new appliances and cars—Mercedes, Cadillacs, Lincolns, Jaguars—all for delivery to the citizens of East Frampton. Maybe even more significantly, the clergy had suddenly left the town. The Congregational minister and his wife left suddenly to tour Europe. The Catholic priest bolted to join the missionaries."

"So," said Flynn. "In this case the shepherds left their flocks."

"Nothing happened until Fourth of July weekend. An unlikely riot broke out in the town. Suddenly, Saturday night, the townspeople attacked the tourists. They routed them out of the guest houses; threw them bodily out of the restaurants and bars; beat them with oars and baseball bats and whiskey bottles—literally chased them up the road to Frampton. Needless to say, the town derived not one penny more from the tourist industry that summer."

"I read about the riot," Flynn said. "Just high spirits on a holiday weekend, wasn't it? Once those things start . . ."

N.N. Zero had continued to place unshelled peanuts in the lions' cage, one by one.

The lioness blinked lazily in the sunlight.

The lion yawned.

"Last Monday," N.N. Zero said, "an air force major, working in a most sensitive Intelligence department at the Pentagon, reported that on Saturday morning he found a manila envelope on the seat of his car, with his name on it. Inside the envelope was one hundred thousand dollars in cash."

"My, my." In the middle of the pavement a shoe-shine boy was kneeling, polishing the shoes of a man in a green suit. The knees of the boy's jeans were torn. "Did anyone else in the department receive a similar Easter basket?"

"Only one other says so—a first lieutenant named DuPont, fresh from Yale."

"I see," said Flynn. "Possibly independently wealthy."

N.N. Zero was still reaching out and placing peanuts in the lions' cage, one by one.

"However," sighed N.N. Zero, "during that weekend, the department's general and one colonel applied for early retirement; the other colonel ordered a twenty-eight-foot Mariner sloop. A technician is known to have eloped. Monday morning, the department's head secretary called in sick, but there was no one at her apartment. . . ."

"We must find out whoever is doing this," proclaimed Flynn, "and give him my address!"

Across the pavement a ragpicker was going through a trash container. Her stockings hung down to one cracked brown shoe, one cracked black shoe.

"Was there a chaplain associated with the Intelligence department?"

"Not specifically."

A middle-aged woman went by them on roller-skates.

"The syllogism wobbles," said Flynn.

"A small town in Oregon went berserk in August. But it was discovered some kids had fed a chemical hallucinogen into the town's water supply."

"Boys will be boys."

"These were girls."

"Girls will be, too."

"Frank, some experiments were carried out during World War II—one nation's trying to flood an enemy nation with false currency. K. has tried it too, as you know, in Israel, Chile, Iran. There was never enough of it to make that much difference."

"That can't be happening here," said Flynn. "A relatively small amount of money, dropped on three points of the compass over a six-month period. Doesn't sound like the handiwork of K. to me at all."

"They could be experimenting. Texas. Massachusetts. Washington. That's what frightens me."

"Are we dealing with funny money?" Flynn asked. "You didn't say that."

"There's a sample in your pocket."

Flynn took the fifty-dollar bill N.N. Zero had given him out of his pocket and examined it.

"That one is from Ada, Texas. The minister sold it to us for another fifty-dollar bill." N.N. Zero handed Flynn a one-hundred-dollar bill and a twenty. "These are from our major in the Pentagon. From him we could appropriate the whole sum."

"Did you give him a receipt?"

"We will, Frank. We will."

"Thank you." Flynn examined the three bills. The thought of sitting down to a New England boiled dinner crossed his mind. "My, my," he said, putting the bills in his pocket.

The lions had not moved in their cage at all. The female had fallen asleep, her head on the male's flank.

The front of their cage was a mess of shelled and unshelled peanuts.

"I'm afraid I'm going to have to keep you away from your cover job with the Boston Police awhile longer, Frank. And from your kids."

Flynn thought of the tall brown Victorian house on Boston Harbor and the noise and other music that came out of it.

Again he felt the desire for a New England boiled dinner.

"We have to find the source of this money," N.N. Zero said. "Who is dropping money—maybe millions of dollars—on unsuspecting people, and why he is doing it. You call me in the morning, Frank, and tell me what you need."

Down to their left, N.N. Zero's three bodyguards stood near an aviary.

"You didn't get your family over to the farm in Ireland this summer," N.N. Zero said.

"There wasn't time. Between one thing and another."

"Putting you up there in Boston, I meant to be putting you on ice."

"I know."

N.N. Zero stood close beside him, which was something the little man seldom did with tall people.

"What do you think, Frank?"

"Well," said Flynn. "I don't think lions like peanuts at all."

4

"Where are you calling from, Frank?"

"Austin, Texas, sir. You told me to let you know this morning what I'll need."

"Shoot." N.N. Zero's voice was as clear as if he were standing next to Flynn. He could have been anywhere in the world at that point, but could still be reached at the same Pittsburgh relay telephone number.

And the line was always scrambled.

"The names of all the citizens of Ada, Texas, and East Frampton, Massachusetts."

"Right. The F.B.I. lifted the town records from Ada."

"The names should be gone through to see if any of their citizens or ex-citizens made themselves particularly wealthy."

"Will do."

"Plus whatever photographs of the citizens of Ada you can develop from old military records, police files, whatever."

"Where do we send it?"

"Las Vegas. Casino Royale. I'll be arriving there in a day or two."

"Any new thoughts, Frank?"

"No, sir. Just don't think we should start an international scare if we're dealing with just one good old boy who's turned generous in the face of the Grim Reaper."

"Find the source of the money, right?"

"You might also have a list of the individuals in this world who have the odd four hundred million mackerels to plop in the sea. There can't be many of them. Inquiries should be made of them."

"You think anyone that eccentric would tell the truth?"

"I don't know he wouldn't," said Flynn. "I've never been that eccentric, myself. I've never had the money."

"What about institutions, Frank?"

"What institutions?"

"Foundations. The mob. Groups that have that kind of money."

"Usually groups have at least one sane person somewhere."

"Take N.N., for example," said N.N. Zero. "Hot down there in Texas?"

"There's a hot wind blowing, and me dressed in the tweeds."

"Keep in touch with Central, Frank."

Randy, one of Flynn's fifteen-year-old twin sons, answered the phone at the house in Winthrop.

Flynn could tell the voices of his twin sons apart.

"Randy, I have a puzzle for you."

"Yes, Da?"

"What could depopulate a town in Texas, cause the people of a resort town in Massachusetts to go berserk and act against their own best interests, and render an important Intelligence department at the Pentagon completely useless?"

"A skunk?"

"Guess again."

"Pollution."

"What kind of pollution?"

"Something in the air? A gas?"

"Guess again."

"Poison. A poisonous gas?"

"Keep working on it. Tell your mother I'll be away for a while. I'll call in whenever I can. If there's an emergency, she should call Pittsburgh."

5

"Would you be the Reverend Sandy Fraiman, by the least chance?"

Even in the wind, Flynn was sweating on the broken front porch of the pitted white house next to the church.

"Yes," said the man through the screen door. His eyes were badly bloodshot.

"I'm someone named Flynn. Sent down here to ask you what happened to this town."

The man pushed the screen door open.

"I'm glad to see anyone," he said.

Flynn followed him into the barely furnished, rugless living room. The drawn Venetian blinds were clattering against the window frames.

Reverend Sandy Fraiman was in his late thirties. He was dressed in a torn T-shirt and new-looking jeans and his feet were bare. His hair and his eyes were black as an ambassador's shoes.

"Tell me," said Flynn. "Is the name Sandy, in your case, a diminutive for the proper name Alexander?"

"No. Why should it be?"

"You mean Sandy was the name given you at birth?"

"Sure."

"Well," said Flynn, "I hope you know your parents had trouble with their eyes. Sandy you're not."

Before Flynn's eyes were adjusted to the light in the dark house, he thought he saw the minister slide a glass under a chair with his toe.

The minister sat in the chair.

"Sit down, Mister Whoever-you-are."

"Flynn," said Flynn.

"It's just this side of perdition, living in an empty town. The Lord be praised. The things He sends to try us."

Flynn lowered himself onto the uncomfortable wooden-framed divan.

"I'll give an amen to that, I will."

Ada, Texas, was empty.

On the long drive from Austin in his rented Plymouth, Flynn had felt the sense of space keenly. Thirty miles from Houston he realized a yellow Fiat convertible was behind him, maintaining exactly his speed, not catching up to him, not falling behind. Twenty miles farther, the car turned off on a ranch road. Through his rearview mirror, Flynn watched its dust rise. For the rest of the way he had nothing to watch but the horizon turning with incredible slowness, the highway remaining as unchanging as a spinster.

Miles from the town of Ada, Flynn had seen evidences of abandonment. Tractors stood out in the open. Front doors and even some barn doors had been left open, blowing in the wind. Cattle lay, their bellies bloated, dead in the scrub pastures and along the road.

Ada's main street (there was only one street), was shut up. The window of the hardware store was cracked and the shades of the grocery store were drawn. The feed store looked locked.

At best, Ada, Texas, had been a boring town.

"The Lord has not abandoned me," said the Reverend Fraiman. "That I know."

"He's left you crying in the wilderness, though."

"The Lord is within every person. In every one of us."

Flynn scratched his head. "Then a lot of the Lord just left town."

Although there were only two of them in this abandoned corner of the world, the Reverend Fraiman raised his chin and spoke to the back of the small room. "No matter how much the messenger of the Lord raises up his people, he must not raise them up in their own eyes. For the Lord is God and He does not love the pride of arrogance. Nor may the messenger, however much he loves his own people, raise them up even in his own eyes. For the Lord is his God and not even God's most wonderful creature, man, may be allowed to obscure the messenger's vision."

A particularly strong wind rattled the Venetian blinds.

"Reverend Fraiman, if you could tell me what happened here, to the people of this town . . . ?"

"Satan came to them in the night, every man, woman, and child of them, and whispered in their hearts that despite all the manifestations of the Lord they had witnessed on this earth, they were his children, the children of Satan, and he filled them with madness, and he stole their souls away."

"The devil took them?"

"As the Lord said . . ."

The reverend's chin remained high, but there were tears in his eyes. He swallowed.

"I'm sure you're right, Reverend Fraiman," Flynn said. "In a way. Sure, the devil took them. And your wife . . . may I ask after her?"

"No, no." There was alarm in the reverend's eyes. "She just drove into Bixby. She has to drive all the way into Bixby just to get the groceries."

"I see." Flynn tried again to make himself comfortable on the broken couch. "I'm sure the people in such a wee town as this come to mean the world to each other."

"Sure."

"Ach, sure, I know," said Flynn. "They grow up together, love each other, hate each other, marry each other, have babies, know well each other's surprising sins, each other's surprising nobilities."

"What did you say your name is?"

"Flynn."

"You're not from around here."

"No," said Flynn. "I'm not. I'm not from anywhere in Texas."

"You like this part of the world?"

"There's a lot of it," admitted Flynn.

"Are you Christian?"

"Well," said Flynn, "I'm workin' at it. Isn't that the most that can be asked of any man, whatever the question is?"

"Have you the gift of tongues?" asked the minister.

"No, sir," answered Flynn. "Only the gift of gab."

"Will you pray with me?"

The reverend's bloodshot eyes stared at Flynn.

"Good Lord, man, what do you think I'm doin'?"

"On our knees, Mister Flynn, we shall join hands and raise our voices in praise of the Lord."

"I'll do my own prayin'," said Flynn, "on my own time."

"Are you saying you will not pray with me?"

"I'm on duty. I'm here, you see, to inquire why the people of this town ran off between a Saturday and a Thursday. Now if you'd only speak to that?"

"Mysterious are the ways of the Lord."

"Reverend Fraiman, if I wanted to inquire into the ways of the Lord, I could have stayed home with my family." Flynn's tweed trousers were sticking to him in the heat. "Now on that Thursday you called the F.B.I., it wasn't to ask them to praise the Lord with you, although I'm sure a dose of the old 'Lead, Kindly Light' would do them no harm, either. I'd be pleased if you'd tell me what you told them, in the greatest detail of which you are capable."

"Aren't you from the F.B.I.?"

"The F.B.I.," sighed Flynn, "wrote out a report of this incident and sent it on to us."

"Then why do I need to go through it again?"

"What?" said Flynn. "Have you never repeated yourself in your life? Then, for all that, you've done damned little what-you-call prayin'." Flynn leaned forward and said more gently, "You may take it, Reverend Fraiman, that the F.B.I. do indeed have the gift of tongues. Their every utterance is magnificent in its power, but mysterious to us poor mortals who cannot keep up with their codes. I'm sure the Lord understands them, but the rest of us are left on our knees, gaping at the wonder of it all. Therefore, if you wouldn't mind giving me the word, I suspect all Israel will hum your praises."

"You're not an ignorant man, Flynn."

"Even at this very moment," said Flynn, sitting back and raising his hand to the ceiling, "I pursue knowledge. Now: about three months ago, you called the F.B.I. office in Austin. Is that right?"

"Yes."

"Had you ever called an F.B.I. office before in your life?"

"No."

"Had you ever met the F.B.I. agent in Austin?"

"No."

"Have you ever called the police for any reason whatsoever before in your life?"

"Yes. Of course."

"When?"

"A year ago. A year and a half ago."

Flynn waited for him to explain.

"Coming home late one night. From a Prayer Day in Austin. I found a couple of dozen kids on the highway. Cars, pickup trucks. I stopped. I realized they were arranging drag races, or whatever. I asked them to stop. Even when I identified myself, they ignored me. This was outside Bixby. There were no Ada kids there. Some were drinking beer, and I saw a whiskey bottle. I stopped at a ranch nearby and called the police. The police in Bixby. I was afraid someone might get hurt."

Flynn said, "You're not a man to call the police every time there's a shadow on the road."

"No," said the minister. "I'm not. There is a higher law. . . ."

"Then calling the F.B.I. was not a small matter to you. . . ."

"My wife and I discussed what I should do many times before I did anything. Before I called Austin. We prayed over it."

"All right now, Reverend: why did you call the F.B.I.?"

"The sheriff was gone, too. He left Tuesday. We saw him leave."

"Were you thinking a crime had been committed?"

"A crime?"

"People are prone to call the police or the F.B.I. when they think a crime has been committed."

"I don't know whether a crime has been committed. A mystery had happened. Everyone in town just got up and left. We wanted the mystery investigated."

"Do you feel the mystery has been investigated?"

"An agent, an F.B.I. agent came down. A nice young man. Named Silvers. Agent Silvers. I told him all about it."

"What did he say?"

"He agreed with me."

"How's that?"

"He agreed it was Satan's work."

"He did, did he?"

"Before he left we joined hands and shared in praising the Lord."

"My God."

"Since then, I have racked my brain and spent

many hours going over the word of the Lord, studying each sample in the Testament of sudden emigrations."

"And what have you found out?"

The minister lowered his head. "I can find no parallel. Here there was no famine, no pestilence. . . . I'm sure there is a lesson somewhere. I've even written the dean of my old school in Alabama."

"What did he say?"

"He didn't exactly write me back. Not yet, that is. He sent me a copy of his new book, *Jesus, I'm Coming.* That was real good of him. I read through it, believing there might be some reference to sudden emigrations, but there wasn't."

"Did the book come with a bill for it?"

"No! Lord, no. I did see the price of the book and mailed him a contribution to cover expenses."

"Mysterious are the ways of the Lord, indeed," said Flynn. "Your Man chased the money changers from the Temple, but so far no one's done anything about those who take advantage of others through the mail. And have you ever heard back from the devout F.B.I. man again, Agent Silvers?"

"Yes, he called once."

"To say what?"

"Well, to say Alligator Simmons had been killed."

"Who was Alligator Simmons?"

"A boy from town. Agent Silvers said he had been shot dead in a bar in Fort Worth."

"In the act of robbery? Was he holdin' up the bar?"

"No, no. Nothing like that. Agent Silvers said it was one of those 'I'm-from-Ada-and-can-whup-anyone-in-Fort-Worth' kind of things."

"He was shot for that?"

"Well, you're not from Texas, Mister Flynn. He said it several times runnin'."

"And someone shot him?"

"In Texas, they call that *lookin' to be shot.* In Fort Worth, especially, that kind of talk is suicidal."

"My, my. I must remember to mind my manners if I'm ever in Fort Worth."

"Alligator was carrying a gun."

"Why was he carrying a gun?"

"You wouldn't go into a bar in Fort Worth and say that kind of thing unless you were carrying a gun."

"I believe Texans have a most refined sense of suicide," mused Flynn. "And tell me, how old a boy was this Alligator?"

"Fifty. Fifty-two maybe."

"Fifty-two! He got a skinful, stood up on his hind legs, and bellowed bravely for three minutes runnin' —and someone shot him?"

The minister's bloodshot eyes bulged, but he said nothing.

"And did you ever hear anything else from Agent Silvers?" Flynn asked in a milder manner.

"No," the minister answered. "Two other men came down and took the town records from the sheriff's office. They didn't say much."

"Did you get them on their knees?"

"What did you say?"

"Never mind. The sound of the wind tires a body out, doesn't it just? Now, if you'd just tell me what you told Agent Silvers in the first place . . . ?"

"Sure."

"Whew. Hot enough, too."

Flynn tried to pick the tweed away from his legs.

"Saturday—all of three months ago, now—I went to see Billy Pat, sayin' the Lord had blessed us and I was prepared to engage him and his men to spruce up the church. The foundation's cracked. . . ."

"If you'd begin at the beginning," said Flynn, "we'd get to the end faster."

"The beginning?"

"You and your wife rise up from the sleep of angels . . . at about what time?"

"We got up at six-thirty."

"You buckled on your toast and coffee. . . ."

"We came to the living room, knelt. I read a chapter, she read a chapter, I read a chapter."

"On your knees?"

"Of course. We joined hands and sang a hymn. We said the Lord's Prayer together." The minister blushed. "Then we kissed and wished each other a good day. This is a Christian home, Mister Flynn."

"Then you had breakfast."

"My wife went to get the eggs, while I tidied the bedroom and the bath."

"You mean, she went out for eggs? She went to the store?"

"She went out to the hens. We have hens. We try to save as much as we can. This is a poor community, Mister Flynn. My wife and I don't feel we should be any more of a burden to the people here than we need to be. It's a good example. What would the people think of us if we lived off store-bought eggs? We try our best at raising our own vegetables too, but—" The minister shrugged.

"What was the first unusual thing that happened to you that morning?"

"Unusual?"

"Out of the ordinary."

"The first? Well, I don't know. Well, yes, I do know. Marge tripped on the back stoop. An egg fell right out of her apron."

"It broke," guessed Flynn.

"It was almost useless. She was deeply vexed with herself. She called the Cranins' dog, from next door, and he came over and lapped it up. To do her penance, Marge went to sweep off the front porch before putting a thing on the stove for breakfast."

"And all this time, you were scrubbin' the tub, waitin' for the odor of coffee."

"I heard Marge call me. She was standing in the front door, broom in one hand, two big manila envelopes in the other. 'Someone must have left these for us,' she said. 'My name's on one.' I took one envelope from her, causing her to drop the other one. It fell on the floor, and all this money spilled out."

"What was your first reaction to that?" asked Flynn.

"Praise the Lord, Mister Flynn. We both said, 'Praise the Lord.' We sat at the kitchen table and counted the money."

"What," said Flynn. "Before breakfast?"

"There were two hundred thousand dollars in the envelopes, Mister Flynn."

"I'm hearin' it's as difficult to get to breakfast around your house as it is mine. Did you eat then?"

"We knelt and praised the Lord. Joy was in our hearts."

"Then you had breakfast?"

"After breakfast, I drove over to see Billy Pat."

"Wait a minute, Reverend Sandy Fraiman. Did either you or your good wife ever stop and ask yourselves, or each other, where the hell the money came from? It's not every morning you wake up and find a pot of gold on the front porch, now, is it?"

The minister's answer was definite. "It came from the Lord, Mister Flynn."

"I see. I wish I could get you to swear to that."

"I will. Happily. On the Lord's Word."

"So you zip out to see the construction man, to see about shorin' up the church . . . ?"

"Yes. Billy Pat. But he wasn't there. And that surprised me some, I'll tell you. I mean, Billy Pat might have been out on a job, although he hadn't had any jobs lately, that I know of—you know, once in a while Billy Pat would get the job of goin' out to dig a well, but that was only in sort-of good times, when people had money to be optimistic. But Bea, his wife, was—well, blessed by the Lord with too much weight, and she hardly ever left that chair of hers on the front porch. And they had four teenaged kids, you know. No one was around at their place.

"Well, drivin' over to Billy Pat's I noticed that the gas station was doin' a land-office business. People were still crowdin' around the gas pumps when I was drivin' back.

"So I stopped and got out of the car to tell the people the good news. 'Praise the Lord!' I said. 'Praise the Lord!' And I told them about the money the Lord had delivered unto us to repair the church and that the next morning, Sunday, the service would be a service of praise and thanksgiving."

"And what did the people say to that?"

"They seemed happy. I told them to pass the word. And they said they sure would."

The minister, looking at his hands folded in his lap, shook his head sadly.

"Marge spent the day on the phone, passin' the word. Calling out around the ranches. As the day went on, more and more people weren't answerin' their phones. 'That's odd,' Marge said. 'Let me try the Bronsons. They have a sick old daddy and I just know they can't all leave the place at once.' She called the Bronson spread and, would you believe, no one answered?

"In the afternoon, we started seein' the cars and pickup trucks goin' by, goin' both directions, loaded up with mattresses, big family clocks, television sets, people. Marge and I couldn't make it out. We worried there was a prayer meeting somewhere we hadn't been called to. Why else would people be leaving Ada all at once? Where else have they got to go? Marge said the people wouldn't be bringing family clocks and mattresses to a prayer meeting, least no prayer meeting we ever heard of. It was the wrong season for football, I said.

"Next morning, Sunday, the town was very quiet. I went over to lead the service, Marge with me, and would you believe there were only about twenty people in the church? That hadn't happened before. Not since I was called to this church, eleven years ago. Many, many people in this town, Mister Flynn, have been born again, have accepted new life in the spirit of Jesus Christ, have—"

"You were surprised there were so few attending service," Flynn urged him on.

"And those who came weren't coughin' or sniffin'. I mean, there was no sickness around. We thanked the Lord anyway. We were real sorry the whole community wasn't there, though, so the Lord would hear one voice, raised in—"

"What did you and Marge do then? Did you talk to the people?"

"We tried, we tried. No one seemed to have any more time for us that morning. Why, we came back to the house and prayed for what understanding the Lord would give us."

With his handkerchief, Flynn wiped some of the sweat from his neck.

"Well, the traffic was picking up again, and Marge and I went into the street and began stopping the pickups. 'Where y'all goin', Louise?' 'Well, we're just goin' in to Dallas to visit with Frank's brother's family, you know?' 'Where you going, Tom Coffey?' 'I been called to Las Vegas, brother. Visit a sick friend.' 'Jack and Mary Lou, now where you takin' these nice children of yours?' 'Well, you know, Marge, they ain't never seen the ocean. This land of ours is so parched. We're goin' to show them the Pacific off California.' 'What're you doin' about your animals?' Marge began askin' every one of 'em. 'Who's takin' care of your critters?' She never got one answer to that question.

"Dusk came, and there was ol' Marge standin' in the middle of the street, sayin' to no one, 'What're you doin' about your animals?' Then Marge began to cry."

Flynn listened to the wind. He heard it building far away. From what he had seen of Texas, there was nothing to stop the wind.

"There was no understanding this, for us," the Reverend Sandy Fraiman said. "Next morning, we drove around to the ranches we knew were empty. No one was taking care of the animals. They had been just left. We went from ranch to ranch, tryin' our best to feed and water 'em. We just couldn't understand what had gotten into these people. What had Satan said to them? How had he appeared? Well, we worked until three o'clock Tuesday morning, when we had to come home. Exhausted. Next morning we started out again. Grocery store was closed. Sheriff's office was locked. Feed store. Few people were around, and I'll swear, those few left because everyone else in town had. We kept tryin' to feed the animals all that day and night. We knew we couldn't save all the animals around Ada. Why, we didn't even know how some ranches in Ada worked their water. Thursday, after prayer, I called the F.B.I. Was I wrong?"

"No," answered Flynn. "You were right."

"What could I do?"

"Still no one told you why they were leaving town?"

"Oh, they told us why, all right. They wanted their kids to see the ocean. What they didn't say was how they could leave. How could they leave their homes, their ranches, their animals? How could they so fall in with Satan?"

"Have you any answer to that?"

"No," said the Reverend Sandy Fraiman. "I don't."

"What, then?" said Flynn, the sweat dribbling down him.

"What, then? Well, I called some of the preachers around here I know and tried to tell them what happened. It must have sounded crazy, it must have— tellin' 'em everybody in Ada had run off their places leavin' all their animals. It took some convincin'. Preachers in the other towns organized some ranchers and sooner or later they came over and took most of the animals off, the healthy ones anyway, to keep 'em fed and watered. They're supposed to return 'em to the people of Ada, if and when they ever come back. They'll see some feed bills then, you bet your life. . . . I expect—well, I know, the people from the other towns took some stoves and a few tractors and like that, for collateral, I guess, against the feed bills."

"The town has been plundered," asserted Flynn.

"I was thinkin' on the animals," the minister said uncomfortably. "I know the grocery was broken into."

Flynn heard a car.

"What else was I supposed to do?"

Flynn said, "I don't know."

"Everybody in town left."

"Everybody?" asked Flynn. "Absolutely everybody?"

"Well, no. There's the pig woman."

"Pig woman?"

"Old Mrs. Lewis. She's a poor thing. Blessed by the Lord with her own craziness. She runs pigs in a gully just west of town."

When the minister heard the car he looked alert.

He said, "That must be my wife. Marge."

Suddenly he got up and went into the kitchen.

The kitchen was quiet.

Flynn heard the car door bang.

He got up and stepped quietly so he could see into the kitchen.

The Reverend Sandy Fraiman was on his knees on the kitchen floor, shoving a nearly full bottle far back behind some cereal boxes.

6

"**B**ut what about the earthquake?" she asked. "Did you tell Mister Flynn about the earthquake?"

"I said there was no earthquake!"

"I felt the tremors, Sandy. I surely did."

"There was no earthquake!" Standing barefooted in the yard between the house and the dusty old car, the Reverend Sandy Fraiman raised his hand to the sky. "That was Satan walking! He has walked in this land!"

Marge Fraiman searched Flynn's eyes for understanding.

She was a slip of a woman in a long cotton dress hanging from her breasts, showing little of her white, skinny legs. Her hair was pulled back and clasped. It gave her a particularly drawn, tired look.

Fraiman had introduced Flynn as she came through the back door with a bundle, then told her rapidly, nervously about what he had told Flynn as he went back and forth to the car, bringing in more bundles.

In the kitchen, Marge Fraiman said, "I'll bring you around, Mister Flynn. Show you what an abandoned town looks like."

"We can take my car," said Flynn. "You might enjoy the air conditioning."

"First we'll go to the grocery store," she said. "We can walk there."

Leaving the minister to his unpacking, they walked through the small house and out the front door.

As they crossed the main street of Ada, Texas (population formerly 1,856; presently three, including the pig woman), Flynn said to her: "Earthquake?"

"Well, I thought so. I surely did." They avoided a scrub pine lying in the middle of the road. "Of course I didn't recollect it until all this had happened—after our brothers and sisters left and we were scratching our heads as to why on earth they'd do such a thing."

"When do you think you felt the tremors?"

"Why, that Thursday morning before—you know, before everybody began pullin' up stakes? That Thursday morning, real early it was, and late the night before, Wednesday."

"What were the tremors like?"

"The earth moved. Just as if Satan was walking the land."

"Mrs. Fraiman, did anyone else mention to you feeling the tremors?"

"Why, no. I scarcely gave it a thought myself, at the time."

The front door of the grocery store had been forced open crudely—most likely with a well-aimed kick.

Flynn said, "I take it the tremors you say you felt were not enough to make you think of moving away from town."

"No. But you never know. The other people might have felt them more than I did. The tremors might have given them more worry than they did me. My husband says he didn't feel them at all."

Behind the door of the grocery store, on the floor, lay a dead cat.

"Poor Bowie," said Marge Fraiman. "We forgot all about you, didn't we?"

Except for a few cans that had dropped and rolled into corners, the shelves were bare. A half-empty box of crackers was on its side on the checkout counter. Someone had stepped on a cereal box in the main aisle.

Heads of lettuce were rotting in their bins and on the floor.

Tomatoes had been thrown against the wall.

"Poor Mister Joe Barker," Marge Fraiman said. "He just worked so hard at keepin' this store. Who'd ever think he'd run off? And him in his middle seventies."

"I expect people in this town found it hard to keep up with their grocery bills?" Flynn asked.

"They surely did. We all do. Are you a family man, Mister Flynn?"

"I am."

"Then you know the price of things. Isn't it just wicked, the way the price of things has just skyrocketed?"

"It is indeed, ma'am."

She had picked up a loaf of stale bread. "Just look at the price marked on that. My mommy would roll over in her grave, if she knew what we're expected to pay for a loaf of bread just now. Sometimes I can't help but think, Mister Flynn, that somehow we're bein' had."

" 'Had,' ma'am?"

"Well, the price of things. Just look. I suppose if you have a good salary, you just get used to it."

"No, ma'am."

"The farmers and ranchers aren't makin' that kind of money. They produce the food. Don't get much for it. How come the food costs so much when you buy it in the store?"

Flynn said nothing.

Marge Fraiman put the loaf of stale bread carefully back on the shelf, as if she had decided not to buy it.

35

"Of course, the people did get squeezed, you know. Well, they got squeezed."

"How do you mean?" he asked.

"Well, because of inflation. They heard their farms and ranches went up two or three times in value so they all rushed off to the bank and raised their mortgages as high as they could, and went off and bought all this equipment on credit, these huge tractors, air-conditioned, some of 'em, combines, washers, dryers. Why, Raury Phil had three tractors out to his place, and his daddy had run the same place with nothing like a tractor. Never could keep up the payments. Every other week he was runnin' into Bixby to up his mortgage some more, just to pay the credit charges. Some of these people around here were in real trouble, Mister Flynn."

Flynn stood ready to pull the door closed after them.

She looked around the store. "I suppose I should come over here and clean up, one of these days. Someone will want this store. I don't know whether it will be Mister Joe Barker, or not. I believe one of his grandsons is in Wyoming now." She looked again at Bowie at her feet. "I don't know how we'll ever get all these animals buried."

The scrub pine had blown about a meter along the street.

After Marge Fraiman was settled in the passenger seat of the car and had said, "My, that's nice," when the air conditioner went on, she offered, "I'll show you the Spaulding place. That will mean something to you."

As Flynn drove, she said, "Now the Spauldings, Helen and Parnell, had to be the most sensible people you ever did know. Born and bred right here. Well, Helen, you know, was daughter of Joe Barker, whose grocery store we were just in? She married Parnell Spaulding just out of high school, and they've been workin' his daddy's place nearly ever since. Mister

Spaulding, Parn's daddy, died early, from smoking cigarettes. We prayed over him, all right. But you'll see this is one of the best pieces of land in these parts. Down here. To the left."

Flynn turned onto a dirt road.

"Look at that," Marge said. "The men who took the cattle left the fence gates open. Well, why not, I suppose. Nothin' to keep in. Nothin' to keep out. Just leave the place to the wind."

Flynn parked beside the house and got out of the car and looked around.

Thirty meters away from the house there was what could have been a streambed next to a tall tree.

Marge said, "Real pretty, isn't it?"

Flynn looked at the house: a small, white, wooden frame building with a deep front porch.

"When we first came here to feed the animals, Sandy put Parn's big new tractor in the barn. He left it sittin' out right there, and just last year at this time he was as proud as a peacock at havin' that new tractor. Your hair would gray considerable, if you knew how much cash money he had to put down to have it." She looked toward the biggest outbuilding. "I wonder if it's still there. I mean, the tractor in the barn."

"Shall I go look?" Flynn asked.

"No." She turned toward the porch steps. "I don't want to know."

Opening the front door of the house, Marge said, "Sandy and I never did come in the house, while we were out here doin' for the critters."

It did not surprise her that the front door was unlocked.

Immediately she went down the passage to the kitchen.

"Look at that," she said.

The kitchen sink was on the floor, leaning against a wall.

"Lord have mercy," she said in awe. "They took the good copper piping."

"What?"

"This was one of the few places around here that had copper piping. They took it! Can you imagine? Look at that! Helen's washer and dryer are gone . . . even that yellow kitchen table she bought over at Bixby two years ago."

There was one wooden kitchen chair knocked over on the floor.

Flynn stood it up.

"You mean, the Spauldings took all this stuff with them, including the pipes?" Flynn asked.

"They surely did not."

Marge Fraiman sat on the chair and looked around the kitchen. "The refrigerator's gone!"

On the windowsill was a plant that had gone brown.

"You know, Mister Flynn, some years ago when Helen Spaulding was having some trouble carrying her fourth child, and we were all worried some, she said something to me I'll never forget. Sandy and I and some others of us had been in to Austin to hear the Reverend Billy Graham, and wonderful that was. Helen hadn't been able to come. Feelin' poorly. When we came back we were all especially full of the Lord, and were talkin' it up in front of her, our joy, and how many we had seen come forward and accept Jesus.

"And quietly, she said to me, 'You know, Marge, I've never felt the need to be born again. I was born into the spirit of Jesus, and surely I've never strayed. . . .'" Marge said: "The bread box is here. Oh, where on earth has that Parn taken her?"

Flynn wandered into the living room and looked around. The carpeting was gone, a divan, at least one other chair. There was no television. He glanced at the five or six titles in a corner of a bookshelf. They were all inspirational, except one: *Plains Poetry*.

Marge Fraiman had come into the room and stopped in her tracks. Her eyes were huge and staring at the bookshelf. Her hands were gripping each other. Her lower jaw quivered.

"Jesus," she said.

Flynn followed her eyes to where she was looking.

"They left their family Bible," Marge said. "Our Lord Jesus. Helen and Parn Spaulding went off and left their family Bible."

It was flat on the bookshelf.

Flynn opened the old volume carefully.

"Look." She came to him and took the Bible from his hand and turned a few pages to show him handwriting. "The whole family history," she said. The entries went from large copperplate to stunted ballpoint. "Their births, baptisms, marriages, deaths."

The earliest date was 1837.

A tear fell on the hand of the minister's wife.

She closed the Bible.

"Mister Flynn, I wonder if you'd mind takin' me home now?"

"I'd be pleased," he said.

She stumbled on the step down to the front porch.

He put his arm around her shoulder. At first, her body tightened and she started away from him. Then she relaxed.

She sobbed once.

"Are you Christian?" she asked once they were back on the highway.

"I'm workin' at it," he said. "And aren't we all, though, whatever we believe?"

Her hands worried each other in the lap of her cotton dress.

She said, "I know my husband's a drinkin' man, Mister Flynn."

He looked at her, small against the car door.

"I see."

"He was a drinkin' man when he got the word in Alabama."

"He must have been very young."

"He was young. The army had him eighteen months in jail for something the drink made him do in Georgia. He came to us in Ada after his schoolin' and I married him. Once or twice he's gone to drinkin' . . . when we began to learn the Lord did not mean for us to have children. . . ."

Flynn said, "He's a good man, Mrs. Fraiman."

"He has the devil in him. That I know."

"Show me someone who doesn't."

"His faith means a lot to him, Mister Flynn. His faith means a lot to me."

"I understand."

"Sometimes I think his faith is wild. Satan didn't walk this land and take these people away."

"What did?"

"I don't know."

Flynn had learned, driving from Austin, that in Texas there was little driving to do. He sat at the wheel while the car took them along the flat, straight road.

"Why do you stay here yourselves?" Flynn asked. "The town is abandoned. The people are gone. Three months are a long time without people."

"He won't go," she said. "He keeps saying the people will come back. He says they will need him more than ever then."

"Three months is a long time."

"Will you pray with him, Mister Flynn?"

"I want to drop you off," said Flynn, "and go see the pig woman."

"Mrs. Lewis."

"Yes."

"She lives out the other side of town anyway. Just keep goin'. You'll see a messy gully off the road down to the left. Start lookin' just beyond Bob's Diner."

"Tell me about Mrs. Lewis."

"Oh, she's a poor old critter. Blessed with madness. A widow lady, I guess. I never remember hearing anything about a Mister Lewis. There used to be some story around that she had a son who went off to New York or South America or someplace and became real rich. She's just been out there in that gully with her pigs since before I was born. What do you call her? A recluse? A hermit? She's been an old woman since I was a child, too. Wonder she's still goin'. Old Mrs. Crazy Lewis."

A yellow Fiat convertible was parked on the main street in Ada. Its top was down.

Flynn slowed to steer around the scrub pine in the middle of the street and to look at the person in the convertible.

"Now, who could that be, I wonder?" Marge Fraiman said.

A woman was in the car, her blond hair just slightly darker than the yellow convertible. She was slumped comfortably in the driver's seat. An open, oversized peppermint-striped collar was either side of her chin.

She appeared to be sketching on a pad of paper placed against the steering wheel.

"Some looker," Marge Fraiman said. "She must be from Dallas."

Flynn stopped in front of the Fraiman house to let her out.

"I'll be back," he said. "In about an hour. After I see Mrs. Lewis. I'd like to talk to you both again, if I may."

"You come on back," Marge Fraiman said. "We'll be here, I guess."

7

Mrs. Lewis was standing so still in the yard when Flynn drove in, he wasn't sure at first she was a person.

She remained standing still after he stopped the car. She gave no indication of knowing someone was seated two meters away, staring at her.

Mrs. Lewis was dressed in a pink evening gown. Her hair was henna'd some shade between red and pink. Her thickly cosmeticked face was as red as the setting sun, except for the large areas of blue eye shadow and the long, dark, heavy eyelashes. Her lips were a slash of heavy crimson. Her necklace and bracelets were sparkling in the sun.

The slightly dirty hem of her ball gown was moving in what wind there was in the gully (not enough for Flynn's olfactory sensibilities), but the rest of her rig was spotless.

Pigs, having set up an alarm when Flynn drove in, now were snuffling around the yard, most keeping to the shade.

There were also many cats in the landscape, in the shade of the sheds, on their roofs, on the windowsill of the shack where Mrs. Lewis apparently lived. The shack was showing its tar paper.

"Praise the Lord," Flynn said to himself.

Getting out of the car, he looked up at the highway. The yellow Fiat that had followed him from Ada was parked on the shoulder of the road.

The pig woman remained unmoving as Flynn approached and stood in front of her.

"Mrs. Lewis?"

She snapped her eyes on his.

The woman must have been near eighty. Her mouth was sunken: toothless. Sweat beaded the cosmetics below her hairline.

Flynn said, "Mrs. Lewis? About three months ago a package was left here, with your name on it. A large manila envelope. May I have it, please?"

The woman's eyes glanced at her shack.

Immediately, she lifted the hem of her ball gown with both hands and daintily made her way across the muck and the mud of the pig yard, up the two board stairs of the shack, and went inside.

Immediately she reappeared in the doorway, a large manila envelope under her arm.

Still holding her hem up, she picked her way back to where Flynn was standing.

She handed the envelope to him, again searching his eyes.

Flynn looked inside the big, bulky envelope.

He didn't need to count it.

The envelope held one hundred thousand dollars in cash.

He smiled and handed it back to her.

"Sorry, Mrs. Lewis," he said. "Wrong envelope."

8

"**N**ow, then." Outside Ada, Texas, Flynn folded his hands together on the counter of Bob's Diner. "What herb teas do you have to offer me today?"

The wasted-looking counterman looked at Flynn as if he were wearing a space suit.

"A little kappa, perhaps?" Flynn asked. "No?"

The counterman slid a greasy, finger-stained menu under Flynn's hands.

"Hyssop?"

Down the counter sat three young men in wide leather belts and jeans. Their motorcycles were outside.

They had been staring silently at Flynn since he'd entered.

In front of each was a can of beer.

"Sure, now, you must have dandelion root?"

"Coffee," the counterman said. "Tea, if you want it. You want a hamburger?"

Coming up out of the pig woman's gully, Flynn had passed the parked yellow Fiat convertible without looking at its driver. He knew she would follow him.

He had driven only a short way before pulling off the highway into the diner's parking lot.

"I could do with a glass of water," Flynn said. "Is your water fresh today?"

The girl came through the door behind him and sat on the counter stool next to him.

The jaws of the three young men fell slack at the sight of her. One could have played marbles with their eyes.

"A glass of water for my friend here, too," Flynn said to the counterman. "Or you might bring us one large glass of water and two straws, we've been together that long, we have."

Keeping his eyes on Flynn, the counterman went to get the water.

"You're Flynn," the girl said.

She had one brown eye and one blue eye.

"Am I?"

"Francis Xavier Flynn. N.N. 13," she said. "Believed by most of your friends and your enemies to be dead."

"They might be right." Flynn ran his hand over the sweat and grime on his face. "At that. One should hesitate before correcting one's enemies."

One of the young men down the counter said, "Pretty lady. Uh! Uh! Uh!"

"I'm Ducey Webb." She took a piece of paper out of the deep pocket of her skirt and handed it to Flynn.

He drank his water before looking at the paper.

> Office of the President
> The White House
> Washington, D.C.

Flynn—

This is to introduce Ducey Webb to my favorite assassin. Discussed this Texas-Massachusetts-Pentagon mystery with Atty. Gen. Agree situation is so curious it must be thoroughly investigated. However, as it is most likely a domestic matter, we would feel less than responsible having it investigated solely by N.N.—an international private organization. Therefore, please work with Ms. Webb, who has carried out successfully many delicate investigations at and for the Justice Department. Atty. Gen. assures me she is tops. Again, thanks for "killing me" without causing me public embarrassment.

The note was handwritten and neither signed nor initialed.

Flynn folded the paper and handed it back to her.

"He writes a nice letter," Flynn said, "doesn't he?"

Ducey put the note back in her pocket.

Flynn said, slowly, looking at her, "It will be nice knowing you, Ms. Ducey Webb."

"I haven't had much briefing," she said.

Flynn drank her water.

"Uh! Uh! Uh!" said the young man down the counter.

The face of one of the other young men was beet red.

"What do you know?" Flynn asked Ducey Webb.

"Not much," she said. "I know that three months ago the town of Ada, Texas, became depopulated, over a four- or five-day period. That a resort town in New England closed down, chased its tourists away, and yet still seems able to pay its bills. And that an entire Pentagon Intelligence section has had to be replaced. Someone seems to be dropping one-hundred-thousand-dollar cash packages on people indiscriminately."

"Indiscriminately?" said Flynn. "I don't know."

"What could the pattern be?" asked Ducey. "What do the three areas have in common?"

"You're ahead of me, Ms. Webb," Flynn said. "I'm not thinking in terms of there being a pattern yet. First, I'm trying to establish that everyone in Ada,

Texas, did receive a package with one hundred thousand dollars in it."

"Have you established that?" she asked.

"Well, I know it wasn't only the minister and his wife who were so favored. The lady I just visited, down in the gully, she who tends her pigs in an evening gown, received a similar package. If Mrs. Lewis wasn't forgotten by the mysterious benefactor, it's doubtful anyone was."

Arms folded over his chest cavity, the counterman was continuing to watch Flynn. He had not refilled the water glasses.

"Then the next question," Flynn said, "is why everyone in Ada, Texas, received one hundred thousand dollars?"

"I know you talked with the preacher and his wife," Ducey said. "What's their explanation?"

"Their explanation can be reported easily," Flynn said. "Their one-hundred-thousand-dollar packages came from the Lord. Everyone else's one-hundred-thousand-dollar packages came from the devil."

"Not much help," she said.

"Not all that much." Flynn moved his glass forward and spoke to the counterman. "Here. Could we have more water, please?"

The man seemed to consider the request before fulfilling it.

Flynn said, "It seems everyone in Ada, Texas, received a package with one hundred thousand dollars cash in it."

"But, Flynn, is that all? Is that enough to make people pull up stakes, leave their homes, their ranches, their cattle, their friends?"

"I think so." Flynn drained his water glass.

"Come on. These ranches are valuable. Some must be worth hundreds of thousands of dollars. People's homes."

"Funny things have been happening to money," Flynn said. "Since I've been in Texas I've heard the expression 'cash money.' There's money and there's cash money, apparently."

"The equipment they own. A combine these days costs more than fifty thousand dollars."

"Remember, Ducey Webb: each person in town received one hundred thousand dollars in cash. One hundred thousand for Papa Bear, one hundred thousand for Mama Bear, one hundred thousand for each child bear, and only the pig woman didn't care. A husband and wife with two kids therefore received four hundred thousand dollars. That's cash money. All spendable. No taxes need be paid on it, if they keep quiet about it."

"Still, Flynn . . ."

"You've seen Ada, Texas?" Flynn asked.

"Yeah . . ."

"Suppose you were a poor old boy workin' your butt off out here, scrubbin' around in this earth for no good reason except that you were born to it, ranchin' a piece of land because someone once told you it was your land, but in truth you're mortgaged to the hilt and the banks have come to own the land you're breakin' your back over, and they also own your tractor and your truck and your living-room chair. Because people have been sellin' you credit so long every year you're paying more and more interest, all your costs are going up, through interest payments, increasing taxes, inflation, what you regard as money makes less and less sense to you. And then one morning you find four hundred thousand dollars cash money outside your front door. Now, tell me, Ms. Webb, what would you do? Give half of it to the government in taxes and the other half to the banks and go back to mendin' your fences, still makin' a tough living, still in debt? Or would you decide to go 'see what other suns and moons there are,' to borrow a line from a play whose name I forget?"

Flynn drank her water.

"We're all in prisons, Ms. Webb. There aren't many

of us—just the preacher and the odd eccentric—who doesn't believe the key to letting us out of that prison is money. Cash money."

"I was warned about your philosophical moments." Ducey Webb grinned.

"I call it thinkin', myself," said Flynn.

"You just said that cash is enough to justify a whole townful of people running off, leaving their homes, their ranches, their friends. . . ."

"Runnin' off from Ada, Texas, to be specific," Flynn said. "No insult to the old place intended. It's not that bad a place. A man can flap his elbows here."

"Okay, Flynn, if we cut the crap?"

"You're just thirsty," said Flynn, patiently. He said to the counterman, loud enough to be heard by all present, "More water, please."

A young man down the counter said, "More water, please. More water, please." He drawled Flynn's lilt. "What they whisperin' about, Sam?"

The counterman refilled their glasses.

"I've got to admit to you, Ms. Webb, it's an astoundin' idea—someone runnin' around droppin' a hundred thousand dollars in cash money on people. Not the usual thing at all. Not easy to put the mind around."

"You've come to Ada, Texas, Flynn, and established, apparently to your own satisfaction, that everyone in town did receive this money." She too was keeping her voice low. "Can you tell me the direction in which you expect your investigation to go from here?"

"There are two questions," said Flynn. "Who is being so generous? Why is he, or are they, being so generous? It's my fervent hope to have both questions investigated at one and the same time. Obviously, whoever is doing it does not want us to find out who he is. At least not yet. If he's got this kind of money, our boyo benefactor can obviously prevent our finding out who he is for a long time—maybe forever, if he wants. Therefore, I think I must try to discover why he is doing it."

"And how do you intend to do that?"

"By peepin' around the land, Ms. Webb, and trying to discover the results of this astoundin' generosity. Do you understand that at all, or would you put it down with another of your four-letter words?"

"What do you mean, 'the results'?"

"It's a simple enough jump, Ms. Webb, isn't it? Or is my logic in need of overhaulin' by a man with a wrench? If you don't know why someone is doing something, you look to the results of his doing it."

"Sometimes," Ducey Webb said, "people don't get the results they desire."

"Sometimes," said Flynn, "they do."

"You mean you're going to chase the two thousand ex-citizens of Ada, Texas, all over the country—the *world*—and ask them . . . what? 'How are you?' 'What's happening?' "

"I mean to take a samplin'," said Flynn. "A wee samplin'."

"Where are you going to start?"

"Las Vegas. But I wish to speak with the preacher and his wife again, first."

"Would you like to listen to me for a while?" Ducey said. "I have some ideas of my own."

"It's well time you contributed to the conversation," said Flynn, "having entered it with nothing more than a letter from the President and a list of questions."

"My first idea is oil, Flynn. Haven't you thought of oil?"

"I've thought of oil," said Flynn. "Frequently."

"Someone wants this area depopulated."

"That could be."

"Maybe someone knows there's oil under all this land and wanted to get the people off it."

"Not impossible," said Flynn. "But if I were a businessman and I wanted to drill for oil, the last thing I'd do would be to scatter the owners of the land and the oil rights to the four corners of the world. If I were giving the owners all this money, at least I'd want some pieces of paper back, signed, sayin' I had the right to drill for oil on their land while they're off lookin' at the Pacific Ocean."

"Oh." She straightened her back. "But no, Flynn. Through the banks. I mean, you said all the ranches around here have heavy mortgages. Within two months, three months—right about now, probably— the banks would be taking over all these ranches because the mortgages aren't being paid. The owners can't be found."

"I think I see," said Flynn.

"See? First you get the people off their ranches . . ."

"Which cost almost one hundred and eighty-six million dollars."

"Then you buy the ranches from the banks."

"For the value of their mortgages, is that it?"

"Yes."

"Is Ada, Texas, worth that much?"

"The oil under it may be."

"I don't know," said Flynn. "I don't know. Sure, we're payin' a fearful price for oil, aren't we, though?"

Down the counter, one of the three young men— the one who had said nothing—took out a switchblade and began to pick his teeth with it.

They had finished their chili and hamburgers before Flynn had entered Bob's Diner.

The dirty dishes were still on the counter in front of them, as were fresh cans of beer.

Ducey Webb said, "My second theory, Flynn, is that you and I are being diddled."

"How's that? Diddled?"

"Diddled," she said. "The object obviously is to depopulate Ada, Texas."

"It could be, I say again."

"Either because of something that is here . . . or because of something that isn't here."

"No need to take a spanner to your logic," said

Flynn. "But may I ask you—politely enough, mind—what the hell do you mean?"

"Supposing the Government of the United States wanted this area depopulated?"

"For what?"

"I don't know for what. Thermonuclear testing?"

"There's an explosive idea."

"To use the area as a radioactive-materials dump?"

"There's a deeper idea."

There was a crash from the other end of the counter.

A chili bowl was smashed on the floor.

No one—not the counterman, not the three young men—moved to do anything about it.

The four men were watching Flynn.

"We're really cooking up some ideas here," Flynn said. "But tell me, Ducey . . . do I recall the name right?"

"Yes. Ducey."

"Don't you have a letter in your pocket from the President of the United States sayin' the whole thing is a mystery even to the government he runs?"

"It may be a mystery to him. The president has no idea what goes on in most branches of his government."

"But something like this . . ."

"It wouldn't be the first time agencies of the United States Government worked at cross-purposes."

"Indeed it wouldn't," said Flynn. "Indeed not. No indeed."

Flynn took out his wallet and placed a dollar bill on the counter.

"For the water," he said to the counterman.

The counterman approached, staring at the dollar bill.

"I'll see you in Austin tonight," Ducey said.

"What makes you think I'm going back to Austin?"

"Because I saw you leave your hotel this morning

52

without any luggage," she answered. "As I was driving up."

The counterman said, "What's this?"

"A dollar," said Flynn. "For the water."

"Are you insulting me?" asked the counterman.

At the end of the counter, the three young men stood up. They began to approach.

One still had the opened knife in his hand.

"You want more than a dollar?" said Flynn.

He had put his wallet away.

The counterman slid the dollar toward Flynn.

"In Texas, mister," the counterman said, "we don't charge a thirsty man for a drink of water."

"I see," said Flynn.

"Take your dollar."

"I will," said Flynn.

He did.

Flynn stood up and found the three young men standing close to him.

The young man with the knife said, "Where're you from, mister?"

"I guess you could say I'm from Ireland," said Flynn.

"Ireland?" said the young man who had blushed.

The man with the knife said, "I knew you were a stranger, right enough."

"Yeats was Irish," said the blusher. "You know Yeats, the poet?"

"I do," said Flynn. "I mean, humbly, I know his work."

The blusher said:

> *I will arise and go now, and*
> *go to Innisfree,*
> *And a small cabin build there,*
> *of clay and wattles made.*

"Indeed," said Flynn.

The young man who had said "Uh! Uh! Uh!" and

tried to imitate Flynn's lilt said, "G.B.S. was Irish, too."

"G.B.S.?"

"George Bernard Shaw."

"He was," said Flynn. "Isn't it marvelous what Irish ears have made of the English language?"

The man with the knife said, "How do you like Texas?"

"It's a surprising place," said Flynn. "I take it you gentlemen are not from Ada?"

They laughed.

"No one's from Ada," one said. "Not anymore. They split."

"It looked a deserted place," said Flynn. "What happened to it?"

"Everyone up and left."

"But why?"

"Why not?"

Mostly they were looking at Ducey Webb.

"There must be a reason," said Flynn.

"None we know of. They all just up and left."

"This young lady is Ms. Ducey Webb," said Flynn.

The blusher asked, "Are you an actress?"

"No," said Ducey. "I work for the government."

"Get out of here," said the grunter, laughing.

The man with the knife said, "I could tell, lookin' at you, you never did a lick of work in all your days."

"Some looker, though," said the grunter.

Flynn said to the counterman, "I'm sorry about the dollar. May I say thank you to you instead?"

"That would be right nice of you."

Flynn said, "Thank you."

"You all come back real soon, now."

"Thank you," Flynn said. "That would be nice."

In the parking lot of Bob's Diner the young men were starting their motorcycles as Flynn and Ducey were getting into their cars.

The motorcyclist who had put away his knife said, "You all need anything?"

"Like what?" asked Flynn.

"Directions? A place to stay?"

"I think we're all right," said Flynn. "But thank you anyway."

"Don't you need anything around here without hollerin' for it."

"I won't," said Flynn.

Two of the motorcyclists roared out of the parking lot of Bob's Diner.

The third—the blusher, straddling his motorcycle—came over to Flynn's car.

"Have you ever seen a production at the Abbey Theatre?" he asked through the car window.

"I have," said Flynn, over the noise of the motorcycle.

"What have you seen?"

"Well, I've seen a production of Shaw's *Saint Joan,* as a matter of fact. With Siobhan McKenna."

"Ooo, boy," the young man said. "That would be great."

"It was great, in fact."

The young motorcyclist said, "I sure would like to see a production at the Abbey Theatre in Dublin, Ireland, someday."

"Tell me," said Flynn. "Do you write poetry yourself?"

The young man's face again turned red.

"No," he said. "I work in an auto-body shop. In Bixby."

Leaving the parking lot, the motorcycle raised a trail of dust.

9

"**W**e're here, Mister Flynn."

Flynn had let himself into the Fraimans' bungalow, out of the wind, yelling, "Hello? Hello?"

"Come on in."

Marge Fraiman's drawl was even slower than usual.

He found the minister and his wife in their bedroom, sitting side by side on the edge of the bed, holding hands.

They looked like two small children at the side of the playground, left out of all activities.

Except the reverend's eyes were glazed, unfocused, wandering in his head.

The Reverend Sandy Fraiman was very drunk.

"There you are," said Flynn.

Marge Fraiman said, "The devil's in him, Mister Flynn."

"I'd say he has about a liter of the devil in him," said Flynn.

"I'm all right." The minister brushed a fly that wasn't there away from his nose.

"He's backslided," Marge said. "Somethin' terrible."

"I think you can answer my questions better anyway, Mrs. Fraiman," Flynn said. "You said you were born and raised here."

"Yes."

Flynn was looking for a place to sit down.

"Sit anywhere," Marge said.

There was nothing on which to sit.

Flynn let himself down cross-legged on the bedroom floor near the window.

"Well, now." The room was stifling. "Just the few odd questions, Mrs. Fraiman."

The minister, eyes closed, said "Oh-h" and pressed his hand against his stomach.

Marge squeezed her husband's other hand.

"Mrs. Fraiman, as far as you know—has anyone ever mentioned to you or to any of your friends that there might be oil under Ada?"

"Oh, no. I mean, sure. People used to talk about it. Years ago. This area's been surveyed time and again, over the years. Exploratory wells drilled. Well, you can still see them standing. At least one on every ranch. It's been a dream the people have had."

"And oil was never found?"

"Oh, sure there's oil."

"There is oil, you say?"

"Of course there's oil. People know right where it is and how much there is of it."

"No oil," said the minister.

"There's precious little of it, Mister Flynn. That's the point. And what there is of it isn't worth drillin' up. Too expensive, even at current prices."

"I see."

"The companies have always been around here lookin' for oil. Everybody gets their hopes up. The companies always show the same maps and tell everybody Ada oil just isn't worth drilling for."

"But oil companies are able and willing to drill deeper now, aren't they? Aren't they willing to spend more money for less oil?"

"They're still not willin' to spend a billion dollars for a teaspoonful, Mister Flynn."

"Answer me this, then: to the best of your knowledge has anyone been around these parts lately doing new surveys, or drilling new exploratory holes?"

"Not for years."

"Years?"

"Years and years. Not since—let's see, I was in the seventh grade. What's that, nearly twenty years ago?"

"Do you think anyone could have been looking for oil around here without your knowing about it?"

"Mister Flynn, if anyone ever comes into any area of Texas—especially Ada—with even a divining rod, I can tell you the news would travel like wildfire. The ranchers would be all over him."

"Right," said Flynn. "Next question: have you ever heard of a radioactive-materials dump?"

"What is that?"

"I know," said the minister. He did not explain. He burped.

Finally, Flynn said, "Thermonuclear plants produce a certain amount of waste material that is radioactive."

"Oh," she said.

"The powers-that-be aren't sure what to do with this waste," Flynn said.

"Why don't they turn it into something useful?" she asked.

"I'll suggest it. Their best idea at the moment is to bury it deep in the ground—especially in a salt deposit."

"Salt?"

"Yes."

"Why, wouldn't that just ruin the salt, too?"

"I guess it would. Anyway," Flynn continued, "the one or two areas chosen to bury this waste—areas I expect are somewhat like Ada—the people have risen up on their hind legs and yelled *no*."

"I don't understand you, Mister Flynn."

"Has anyone ever mentioned to you or any of your friends, as far as you know, that Ada might be used as a place to bury radioactive wastes?"

"Why, no. Whoever heard of such a thing?"

"The devil," said the minister. "The devil did."

He began to giggle and cry.

"The people can't protest," said Flynn, "if they're not here to do it."

"No such thing," said Marge Fraiman.

"There haven't been any men around here diggin' any holes in the ground the last year or two?"

"Surely not. If there were they'd be taken as oil surveyors and we all would have been over them quicker than flies go to a dead man's eyes."

"Beguiling expression, that," said Flynn. "I must remember to use it myself, one day. When it's appropriate. One other wee question: has any born and bred citizen of Ada, Texas, struck out in the world and done especially well?"

"Well, there was young Dale Hainsfather. Last year, why he had more Boy Scout badges and awards than anybody in Texas. He got a special trip to Dallas for it. All paid for."

"Mrs. Fraiman, I guess when I say anyone who has 'done especially well,' I mean become rich."

"Rich?"

"Very rich."

"Why, of course."

"Who?"

"Tommy Jackson, of course."

"Who?"

"Why, surely, Mister Flynn, you know who Tommy Jackson is, don't you?"

"If I do know," Flynn said, "I forget. If you would refresh my memory?"

"He played for Texas."

"Played what?"

"Football. Quarterback for Texas. Of course, that was ten, twelve years ago."

"That Tommy Jackson."

"Sure. I was sure you'd know. His family moved from here to Austin when he was about twelve years old, but he's always said that Ada's his hometown."

"Did he become rich?"

"Why, he sure did. Even while he was in college, they were givin' him cars. They gave him a Bonanza. A yellow Bonanza. It was in all the papers, at the time."

"But did he become rich?"

"He made a lot of money playing football. You'd never believe how much. He's up North someplace, now. Coach of one of those big state-university football teams." Marge looked at her husband like a child looking into a bird's nest to see if there were any chicks. "Sandy would know which university. I understand you can see Tommy on television once in a while. He always says he comes from Ada, Texas, which is real nice of him, I mean, seein' he left here when he was age twelve and all."

"I guess I'm asking about someone even richer than Tommy Jackson."

"Richer than Tommy? They say he lives in a big house, with a swimming pool. There was a piece about him in *Parade* magazine a few years back."

"I mean someone who went somewhere, discovered oil, put together a big company, owned an airline, a lot of real estate, banking . . . something . . . became a billionaire."

Marge Fraiman's eyes had grown wider.

"No, Mister Flynn. I've never known of anyone like that."

"Never even heard of anyone like that?"

"Well, sure, I've heard of them. We don't have a television and don't believe in cluttering up our minds with magazines and like that. If you can read the Word of the Lord, why read anything else, Sandy says." The minister's head went up and down in agreement. "But I know such people exist. There was that man, Howard Hughes—"

"Right," said Flynn. "Someone like him."

"From right here in Ada?"

"That's the question."

"Why, no, Mister Flynn. Who'd ever think a thing like that? All that money, and women, and flyin' around in the face of the Lord? I surely would pray nothin' like that would happen to anyone from Ada. Not anyone I know."

Flynn stared at her a moment, and then said, "Amen."

"No one like that from Ada, Mister Flynn. I pray the Lord my husband's ministry has been better than that."

"You mentioned that Mrs. Lewis had a son who ran off and became rich?"

"Oh, that. That's just a story about the pig woman. I never laid eyes on any son of hers."

"It could have been long ago. Before you were born."

"Well, it would have been. Of course. Old Mrs. Lewis, why, she's a hundred years old if she's a minute and a half."

"You don't know anything definite about her son?"

"Definite? I don't even know she had a son. People love to make up stories about poor unfortunate critters like that. I mean, here she is, out livin' in that gully with her pigs, givin' herself airs, dressin' up in face makeup and spangly glass to pour slop out to the pigs, so everyone goes around sayin' she has a son rich as Croesus livin' in a mansion on Park Avenue, New York. Just 'cause everyone's always said it doesn't mean it's true."

"I suppose not," said Flynn.

"No. It's just a small town's way of feelin' sorry for her, you know? The poor crazy old woman. No one in this town ever's gotten free and had any money,

61

Mister Flynn. No one, except Tommy Jackson, of course. Why would you ask such a thing, anyway?"

Flynn said, "I think you should know—and I think you should tell your husband when you can—that I believe every man, woman, and child in Ada, Texas, received a package just like yours—with one hundred thousand dollars cash money in it."

"I can't believe that, Mister Flynn."

"Mrs. Lewis received such a package."

"Mister Flynn, there are some things that are to be believed, and some things that are not to be believed. I told you about the earthquake—"

"Satan walked the land," the Reverend Sandy Fraiman said.

Flynn rose from the floor. His knees were stiff.

Still holding her husband's hand, Marge Fraiman said, "I won't walk out with you, Mister Flynn, if you don't mind."

Flynn said, "May I ask what you and your husband are going to do?"

"I'll just sit with him," she said, "until it's time to pray."

"And then what will you do?"

"Why, I said: we'll pray."

"Mrs. Fraiman, you and your husband can't sit here in an empty town. It's been three months you've been alone. I have some experience with what that does to people."

"We have the Lord, Mister Flynn."

"Ach, well. Since Eden, Mrs. Fraiman, it's been a good idea to have some other people around. Can't you at least move into Bixby or Austin? You can keep your eye on Ada just as well from there."

"Why, Mister Flynn, that's a right good idea."

"It is?"

"It surely is. I thank you for it."

"Just an idea, Mrs. Fraiman."

"We never thought of it. We never did. I do thank

you for takin' thought for us. That's right Christian of you."

Just as Flynn was leaving the bungalow, going back into the hot, blowing air, he heard Marge Fraiman call out, "You be sure and come back, you hear? Right soon!"

10

Good evening, ladies and gentlemen.
Why am I saying good evening?
It's three-thirty in the morning!
What are you doing up?
What am I doing up?

Like most audiences at a live performance, the people in the enormous Las Vegas lounge watching the comic Jimmy Silverstein on the huge stage with his hand-mike, listening to him, were eager to be pleased, even at three o'clock in the morning.

Flynn sipped his Perrier and lime.

"Get an education," my mother said. "With an education you won't have to be up at three o'clock in the morning, tiptoeing around the city, quietly collecting other people's garbage."

You heard me right: quietly collecting other people's garbage.

"Get an education," my father said. "With an education you won't have to be up at two o'clock in the morning pulling on your pants to come to work at the bakery."

I should have listened!

Flynn had driven from Ada to the Dallas-Fort

Worth airport and then flown to Las Vegas. He had checked into Caesar's Palace, then checked into Casino Royale. He slept, ate, bought a lightweight suit, four shirts, some underwear, socks, a small suitcase, spent hours in his room reviewing the material sent him from N.N., called the Pittsburgh number with several Information Requests, ate and slept again.

The material sent him from N.N. included the names, ages, photos, Social Security numbers, and biographical sketches of everyone who had worked in Air Force Intelligence Section, anything to do with either East Frampton, Massachusetts, or Ada, Texas.

What are you people doing in Las Vegas, anyway?

Miami's a beach, Hawaii's a beach . . . Las Vegas is a beach, but have you ever tried walking to the water from here?

Deep fried tootsies you get five days before you see even a drunk seagull!

Thus far, in Las Vegas, Flynn had traced the following people from Ada, Texas:

JAMES A. FURTHERER, 19. Furtherer had worked in the Ada Wesgas gasoline station. Furtherer was currently working in a Wesgas gasoline station outside Las Vegas. When Flynn asked him what happened to the one hundred thousand dollars he had received, Furtherer said, "What hundred thousand dollars?"

GABRIEL and ALIDA SIMS, 32 and 31, respectively. Ranchers. Divorced in Las Vegas three weeks previously. Sims was now working as a baggage handler at Las Vegas Airport. Alida had bought a small house on the outskirts of Las Vegas and was unemployed.

RONALD and BARBARA ELLYN, 39 and 43, respectively. Ranchers. Ronald dead on arrival, Las Vegas Sunshine Hospital; fatal gunshot wound believed self-inflicted. Barbara's whereabouts were currently unknown.

JOSEPH BARKER, 58. Grocer. Currently in Alcohol and Drug Center, Las Vegas Sunshine Hospital.

MILTON and JACKIE SCHLANGER, 28 and 25, respectively. Ranchers. Currently living in separate rooms at R.O. Motel. Flynn's evidence suggested Jackie was supporting them both by prostitution.

CHARLES, WILMA, and WILMA AGGERS, 38, 36, and 12, respectively. Ranchers. Currently proprietors of the R.O. Motel. Although the Aggers would not state to Flynn the source of their investment in the motel, they did say they were being investigated by the Internal Revenue Service and feared being sent to prison.

Flynn had also found Parnell Spaulding, 54, but had not yet interviewed him.

Flynn had watched Spaulding play roulette between two and four-thirty the previous morning. Spaulding was alone. His concentration on the game was intense.

Las Vegas is a nice beach, but it's a terrible long walk to the water.

What has Las Vegas got?

I'll tell you what Las Vegas has got.

I'll tell you what you think Las Vegas has got.

Money!

Las Vegas has got money.

I've got money; you've got money.

Isn't it great having money?—as long as we have some other means of supporting ourselves.

Flynn's Information Requests from N.N. included the following:

(1) What are the known values of oil rights in the area of Ada, Texas, including "deep wells"?

(2) Are there valuable oil or natural gas rights in the area of East Frampton, Massachusetts, including offshore?

(3) Has any U.S. agency considered the area of Ada, Texas, as a nuclear-waste-materials dump?

(4) State whereabouts of world's ten top known counterfeiters.

(5) What is the relationship of Captain William

H. Coburn, U.S.A.F.I.S. 11B, with Coburn families of East Frampton, Massachusetts, and Ada, Texas?

(6) Is there a man of extreme wealth, age probably about sixty, whose last name is or was Lewis, originally from Ada, Texas?

(7) Who is Ducey Webb?

So what's money?

What's money anymore?

I'll tell you what money is.

Money is tissue paper.

You might as well blow your nose in it!

You heard about the guy who broke the bank at Monte Carlo—really, he won a fortune—brought the money to Las Vegas and by the time he got here he discovered he had to blow it all on a tuna fish sandwich?

Yesterday a guy put up a tent over his manhole in the street while he was down fixing the sewer pipes.

When he came up at five o'clock there were seven sheiks standing in line, oil money in hand, trying to make a deal for his tent!

You know why you're here?

You're not here because you can afford to be.

You're here because what it cost you to get in doesn't matter anymore!

Twenty dollars you paid to come in and listen to Jimmy Silverstein at three o'clock in the morning.

My mother would die, if she knew this.

Your mother would die, if she knew this.

You remember when money was real? Do you?

Now here we all are in this big sandbox called Las Vegas, playing with money!

Because it isn't real anymore!

Wheeeeeeee!

Tell me honestly, ladies and gentlemen: did you ever think you'd live to see the day when the automobile companies had to recall their stock? I mean their common stock?

Here, kid. Here's a fifty-dollar bill. Go buy yourself an ice cream.

Hey, mister. I'm out of work. Can you spare two hundred and fifty dollars?

Listen, it's all right, ladies and gentlemen.

The President of the United States has just written a short book: How I Saved the World's Economy.

It's available from the United States Government Printing Office for only nine hundred and twenty-five dollars.

Plus eighty-two dollars postage.

Thank you, thank you, ladies and gentlemen. You've been a wonderful audience.

Thank you, and good morning.

"Funny place, America," Flynn said to the Fischbecks of Milwaukee, who had been kind enough to invite him to share their table.

"Funny?" the male Fischbeck said.

"Yes," said Flynn. "In America, the truth gets told in some funny places, in some funny ways."

11

"Mind if I join you?" Flynn asked.

It was four forty-five in the morning.

After again watching Spaulding at the roulette table for a while, Flynn had followed him into the bar area.

Parnell Spaulding was a big man, broad-shouldered, thick-handed, with a face just as baked and creased as the land around Ada, Texas. There was a spot of skin cancer at the corner of his mouth.

Spaulding sat alone in a dark corner, his shoulders hunched over a double straight bourbon.

He looked up at Flynn through exhausted eyes, but said nothing.

Flynn slid into the plastic booth across from Spaulding.

After the noise of the cabaret where Flynn had been entertained by Jimmy Silverstein, the lobbies, the gambling rooms—the sight of expensively dressed and coiffed women everywhere, their fingers filthy from feeding coins to the slot machines from Styrofoam cups —this corner of the nearly empty cocktail lounge was a quiet relief.

"I was in your house the other day," Flynn said to Parnell Spaulding. "In Ada, Texas."

There was no reaction from Spaulding.

"Your cattle's dead or gone. Most of your furniture. Your television. I don't know about your farm equipment. Sandy Fraiman ran your tractor into the barn, but I expect it's gone, too."

Spaulding's eyes grew wide.

"Someone has even ripped the copper piping out of your walls and run off with it."

"The copper piping?" Slowly, Parnell Spaulding shook his head. "The copper piping. Don't that beat all?"

Flynn said, "Your family Bible's still there. On the living-room shelf. Where you left it."

"Yeah," Spaulding said. "We left in sort of a hurry."

"I guess you did."

"Did we really leave my great-granddaddy's Bible?"

"You did."

"Wonder Helen didn't think to bring it along. She allus did take the Word of God as bein' somethin' she was in charge of."

"Everyone left Ada," Flynn said. "Except the Fraimans and the pig woman."

"Well," Spaulding drawled, "no matter how long you spend growin' up in Ada, the old place don't improve none."

"Have you found something better?"

"I surely have. We're livin' in a big suite upstairs. Eleventh floor, if you'd believe it. Good as livin' on a hill. I allus wanted to live on a hill. You can see a piece. No dust. Ever. People bring your meals to you, just as polite as they can be. I don't mind livin' in the air conditioning, either. Why, now I change my shirt just for somethin' to do."

Flynn said, "You haven't asked how the Fraimans are. I just mentioned I saw them."

"Hell, I know how the Fraimans are. He's backslidin' and she's forward-pushin'. That's how they allus get to stay exactly where they are."

Flynn smiled.

"I've known a few preachers," Spaulding said. "If they really believed what they preach they wouldn't have to work so hard at convincin' others. That old Sandy. We sort of let him preach to us as a kindness. Kept him off the bottle. Givin' us damnation kept him from raisin' hell.

"And ol' Marge," Spaulding continued. "She took Sandy on the way you're apt to take a lame dog into the house. Plain ugly girl, growin' up. She became Christian 'cause she needed the company."

Spaulding had had little of his drink.

"What are you sniffin' around for anyway, mister?"

Flynn said, "You have to admit it's a wee bit of a mystery when everyone in a town packs up and leaves within five days."

"I suppose it is," Spaulding smiled. "I suppose it is. You from the Internal Revenue Service?"

"No," said Flynn. "I wouldn't be."

"You're from the government, anyway."

"Actually, I'm not," Flynn said.

"You're just nosy."

"Somethin' like that."

"You have somethin to grab onto?"

Flynn stared at the man across the table.

"I'm sure I'll know what you mean . . . ." Flynn said, "if you give me just a moment. . . ."

"You have a name, mister?"

"Ah, yes," Flynn said. "That. Sure I have."

"You mean to hold on to it?"

"Flynn," said Flynn. "Francis—Xavier Flynn. And, yes, I mean to hold on to it."

"You must be from Washington," Parnell Spaulding said. "You talk like such a damn fool."

"Your father-in-law," Flynn said, "Joe Barker. He's in the alcohol ward at Sunshine Hospital."

"Didn't he just lap it up, though? He came to Las

Vegas plannin' to drink it dry. I told him it was nearly impossible, even for a young Texan. Got to give him credit for tryin', though."

"You knew Alligator Simmons?"

"Sure I know the Gator."

"He was shot dead in a Fort Worth bar."

"Ol' Gator must have opened his mouth that once too many times. Put a pint of whiskey in him and he'd crow. Great one for sayin' he could whup anybody. Gator's allus been that way, ever since Lilly-Ann Wurkers beat the piss out of him in the schoolyard when they were sophomores in high school. Gator got shot dead, huh?"

"You heard Ronald Ellyn shot himself, here in Las Vegas about ten days go?"

"I heard. Helen mentioned something about that to me. Ol' Ron never was sure which end of a gun was which. Look, mister . . . what are ya tryin' to say? You want a drink?"

So far the cocktail waitress had ignored Flynn. She was standing at the far end of the bar, in her G-string and bra and high-heeled shoes, concentrating on counting her tips.

"How are you doing at roulette?" Flynn asked Spaulding.

"I find I like the game."

"Win much?"

"Sometimes. Not much recently."

In two nights—or mornings—Flynn had watched Spaulding lose over seventy-five thousand dollars at the roulette tables.

"It's an expensive game," Flynn said.

"I was doin' all right at first," Spaulding said. "Got way ahead. Thought I'd be able to buy Main Street out there, before I was done. In cash money. I've had two, maybe three big winning streaks since that time, too."

"How much of the six hundred thousand dollars do you have left?" Flynn asked.

Spaulding smiled into his drink. "Whoever said I had six hundred thousand dollars?"

"You have a wife and four kids," Flynn said. "Each of you received one hundred thousand dollars in cash; six big manila envelopes all told: six hundred thousand dollars. How much of it do you have left?"

Spaulding hesitated, sighed, sat back, reached into his pocket, and took out a stack of one-thousand-dollar bills. He counted them on the table.

The waitress came over immediately.

"You want anything?" she asked.

"Go away," said Flynn.

Spaulding said, "Twenty-three thousand dollars."

He put the money back in his pocket.

"That's it?" said Flynn.

"Well, I haven't hit a winning streak lately."

"I guess you haven't. What are you going to do when that's gone?"

"It won't be gone. I had over nine hundred thousand dollars at one point. Cash money. Would you believe it?"

"Tell me, Mister Spaulding: the last three months have you been keeping up the mortgage payments on your ranch?"

Spaulding ran his fingers over his chin. "Why, no. I guess I haven't."

"Where are your wife and kids?"

"They're upstairs, I reckon. Asleep. In the suite. On the eleventh floor."

"I suspect you haven't been seeing much of them lately."

"Well, sure. I sleep and eat in the suite. My son, Parney, seems to be havin' himself a high ol' time. Fast cars and fast women make for a fast time. I've got to tell you, though: you get playin' these games and I don't know what happens to time. It gets all jumbled up. I go out and walk around sometimes, to cool off? Sometimes it's daylight, sometimes it's dark. I wake up at five o'clock in the afternoon. The people in the hotel are real nice, though. You want breakfast and they'll give you breakfast whatever crazy time of day or night it is. You know?"

"I know."

"What time is it now, for instance?"

"It's almost quarter past five in the morning."

"See? Wasn't I just tellin' you that?"

The cocktail waitress had finished counting her tips for the umpteenth time.

"Mister Spaulding, what was the source of the money your family received?"

"I never said we received any money, Mister Flynn."

"Where do you think the money came from?"

Spaulding looked at his whiskey glass for a long time.

"I don't know."

"You have no idea?"

"It was just there, lying outside the front door one fine Saturday morning: six little packages all in a row."

"What's your best guess as to where it came from?"

Quietly, after a long pause, Spaulding said, "I admit . . . I have wondered about it."

A woman was standing next to Flynn. He hadn't heard her approach.

Her hair seemed an unnatural shade of red, even in the dark of the bar. She was wearing a long, white evening gown.

She was staring through the gloom of the bar at Parnell Spaulding.

She looked the plumb American ranch wife and mother worn out by the merciless noise and lights and spirit of Las Vegas. Her fingers were filthy from feeding coins into the slot machines.

Her makeup was smeared. Bulbous tears were before her eyes. Her chin quivered.

"Parn," she said. "Parney's dead. Parney's been killed! That crazy car you gave him . . ." She was

struggling to breathe. "That crazy car! Police . . .
Went off the road, rolled over." She raised her arms
and lowered them, slowly. "Parney's dead! Our boy is
dead!"

The cocktail waitress looked over, snapping her
chewing gum.

Parnell Spaulding had started to get up when he saw
his wife, then froze in his seat. He was staring at her
now as if he were trying to figure something out.

Flynn began to stand up, to slide out of the booth.
Spaulding's hand shoved him hard back into the seat.

Parnell stood over his wife, looking down into her
eyes. Flynn watched. Parnell looked as he had at the
roulette table while calculating odds.

A smile played at the corners of Parnell Spaulding's
mouth. A beam of joy came into his eyes.

"God," he said hoarsely. "Now You owe me one.
A big one. Now, God, You have to let me win."

He pushed his wife aside and marched out of the
lounge. He went back to the central gambling room.

Flynn was out of the booth in time to catch Helen
Spaulding as she fell toward the floor.

After a while Flynn led this woman, who said she'd
been born into the spirit of Jesus and yet had left the
family Bible behind, up to her suite on the eleventh
floor, which was like livin' on a hill.

12

F lynn was surprised to find himself being talked to by a computer's voice.

He had called the number in Pittsburgh that had been left for him at Casino Royale's message desk. He said just one word when it answered: "13."

After a click that sounded like someone aligning false teeth before speaking, he heard: "Information Requests N.N. 13.

"What are the known values of oil rights in the area of Ada, Texas?

"Response: negligible."

"Ach," muttered Flynn. "Bein' talked to by a machine, I am. Not a hello or a how-are-you this fine day do I get."

"Are there valuable oil or natural-gas rights in the area of East Frampton, Massachusetts, including off-shore?

"Response: yes; all such rights have been secured by the Mobil and Exxon corporations."

"How are you yourself," Flynn muttered, "and your mother, the vacuum cleaner?"

The machine continued: "Has any U.S. agency

considered the area of Ada, Texas, as a nuclear-waste-materials dump?

"Response: no."

"And your father, the Broadway taxi?" Flynn asked.

And the machine continued: "State whereabouts of world's ten top counterfeiters.

"Response: Hughie Esbitt, the Yacht Buck, Ville-franche, France; Louise Reynick, Villa Caprice, Etel, Switzerland; Cecil Hill, Dascha 11, Solensk, U.S.S.R.; Melville Himes, 11 Wall Street, New York City; Philip Stanley Duncan, Duncan Farms, Willing, Kentucky . . ." The voice droned on without taking a breath—of course. ". . . Franco Bonardi, Villa Chicaga, Cagna, Italy; Martin Malloy, 0748266, Federal Prison, Marion, Illinois . . ." ("Finally," muttered Flynn.) ". . . Muir Jacklin, care of American Express, Paris, France; Robert Prozeller, Seaview Nursing Home, Methodist Center, San Diego, California; Myron Uhlig, Kokkola, Finland, street address unknown."

"I'll bet you had the same breakfast I had," Flynn said. "Two bolts, a dozen washers, and a glass of lubricating oil."

And the machine continued: "What is the relationship of Captain William H. Coburn, U.S.A.F.I.S. 11B, with Coburn families of East Frampton, Massachusetts, and Ada, Texas?

"Response: no known relationship."

"Thanks a ton, you assortment of junk."

And the machine continued: "Is there a man of extreme wealth, age probably about sixty, whose last name is or was Lewis, originally from Ada, Texas?

"Response: yes; George Udine, businesses, addresses various, currently at Cleary's Mountain, Cleary, Oregon.

"Who is Ducey Webb?

"Response: who is Ducey Webb?"

"Your father was a toaster," said Flynn.

"Thirteen: hold. Zero connecting."

"Nice talking with you," Flynn said to the machine. "Call anytime."

"Who are you talking to, Frank?" N.N. Zero, John Roy Priddy, asked.

"Exactly," said Flynn. "Where did we get the rollicking robot?"

"Do you like it?"

"Rollicking. Some of its jokes and stories are a bit out of school, of course. I wouldn't repeat them to the wife of the local vicar."

"I guess we have some new equipment since you've been working with us full-time."

"Does it have a name?"

"Who?"

"Your rollicking robot?"

"I understand some of the young people on the staff call it Ginger."

"Ginger! That's personable enough. Why Ginger?"

"That's what color it is."

"A ginger robot?"

"It's only as big as a cigar box, Frank. Isn't that wonderful?"

"You compressed brains are a constant embarassment to me," Flynn said to the little man. John Roy Priddy said nothing. Flynn added, "Sir."

"Frank, who is Ducey Webb?"

"That's what I'd like to know. I have my suspicions. Were you listening in on Ginger?"

"Just the last part. I didn't want to miss talking with you. Was any of the information useful?"

"Yes. I got exactly two leads out of it."

"How's Las Vegas?"

"It's not a bad place to live, but visiting here gets under the fingernails, if you know what I mean."

"Frank, what the hell are you doing, anyway?" N.N. Zero could ask some super questions. "Start anywhere. It's early yet."

It was six fifty-six A.M. Las Vegas time. John Roy

Priddy hated sleep. All the horrors came back to him in the vulnerability of sleep.

Flynn said, "I went to Ada, Texas, to establish that the town was abandoned within a five day period by everyone except the minister, his wife, and an eccentric old woman. Everyone else who could creep, hobble, or stamp on an accelerator skedaddled."

" 'Skedaddled'?"

"That's a word we use here in the Southwest."

"It didn't sound either Gaelic or German."

"It isn't. I think I have established that everyone in the town—man, woman, and child—received one hundred thousand dollars in cash money."

"Cash money?"

"I acclimate easily," said Flynn.

"Frank, didn't we know all this before?"

"Actually, not. I'm not absolutely sure we know it now."

"We pretty well knew all that, Frank."

"What I did not know, sir, was whether a crime had been committed. Passing around the cash like old Saint Nick is not generally thought a punishable offense. There are very few chubby old gents with long beards and red suits in the various penitentiaries, I believe."

"I'll check. Has a crime been committed?"

"In my use of the word crime, yes. You see, I'm trying to discover the results of this largesse as a means of discovering why it happened."

"What are the results?"

"Devastating. The minister is disoriented, his wife is worried sick, the grocer is in the drunk tank, someone else shot himself, a young wife has turned to prostitution while her husband pimps for her . . . I just saw a solid-citizen type react to his son's death by challenging God at the roulette table. . . ."

"A tale of woe."

"Admittedly, I chose to trace those citizens of Ada, Texas, who came to Las Vegas, Nevada—as if they were lookin' for trouble. What the tales are of the more stable elements, who chose to go somewhere else, I don't know. But even one little family that stayed out of the casinos and bars and invested their windfall in a motel are scared to death the Internal Revenue Service is going to peck down on them and have them in jail within the hour—because they can't say where they got the money."

"I don't know where this leads us."

"I don't know, either," Flynn sighed.

"You've been concentrating on the human element, Frank—as usual."

"No, I've considered the real estate, too. I can find no practical reason why anyone would want the town of Ada, Texas, abandoned."

"It's been a week, Frank, since you and I talked at the zoo."

"This is a most unusual crime, sir. Unprecedented. Novel, I might say. If you have any ideas . . ."

"I haven't."

"We might pose the problem to Ginger the Rollicking Robot, of course. . . ."

"You're satisfied that in human terms a crime has been committed?"

"In fact, I'm getting a bit angry about it. Whatever whoever meant to accomplish, the results of this largesse are devastating. Better some of these people were knocked out by a bomb. That's the thing I know now I didn't know a week ago."

"You always turn philosophical at the weirdest times."

"I'm a seeker after truth."

"Okay. Seek after truth, Frank, but leave the accumulation of wisdom for after you're retired."

"I'll do that, sir," Flynn said. "I will."

"What do you do next?"

"East Frampton."

"Oh, no."

"I learned something by visiting Ada. I can't be as precise as Ginger in describing it, of course . . ."

"All right. Then what?"

"I'm not sure. But I suspect I'll find myself doing some real traveling."

"Like?"

"Like Solensk, Russia."

"Christ, Frank, getting you in and out of Russia at this point in your life . . . Are you crazy?"

"Solensk's on that damned island, isn't it?"

"Okhotsk. Sakhalin. Whatever it's called."

"Where the seagulls do not stop for lunch."

"Why Solensk, Frank?"

"There's a great counterfeiter who has taken up residence there. Name of Cecil Hill."

"Cecil Hill. So what?"

"Don't you think Solensk, U.S.S.R., is a funny place for a counterfeiter to take up residence?"

"Yes. I do. You're right. But, jeez, Frank, getting you in and out of Russia . . ."

"Believe me, it will be the last thing I do."

"It may be."

"I appreciate your humor, sir."

"You're going to East Frampton, Massachusetts, next because you want to see your family in Boston, right?"

"I might stop by to see what's in the refrigerator."

"I envy you." John Priddy had no family. He had No Name. "I guess you know that. The time element worries me, Frank. This thing in Ada, Texas, happened three months ago. East Frampton, even longer ago."

"No one got worried, though, until it was a few people in the Pentagon who got assaulted with money."

"That's true. Well, I agree. This is a weird one. That's why I assigned you to it. You have the weirdest mind I've ever met. If you can't figure why someone is scattering millions around the country, no one can."

"Thank you, sir."

"If you ever get any hard information, don't hesitate to phone in."

"I won't, sir."

"I'd be delighted to hear a fact one of these days. Any fact."

"The very first fact that comes over the horizon I will whisk away to you with blinding speed."

"I await the moment with bated B."

Flynn said, "My best to Ginger."

13

Ducey Webb was standing in the lobby of the Casino Royale when Flynn stepped off the elevator.

She saw his suitcase.

"Checking out?" she asked.

"I am."

Drily, she said, "You mustn't forget to check out of Caesar's Palace, too—where you're also registered."

"I almost did forget," Flynn said.

She followed him to the cashier's cage.

"You never did go back to Austin," she said, "that night."

"You presumed I was going back to Austin because you saw me leave the hotel that morning without any luggage."

Her one brown eye and one blue eye shifted from his left eye to his right and back again.

"I didn't have any luggage at that point," Flynn explained.

She nodded. "My, my."

Flynn was checking his hotel bill.

"Therefore," she said, "you came to Las Vegas,

checked into one hotel and actually stayed in another just to fool me."

"It took you a long time to figure it out," Flynn said.

Ducey shrugged. "Your room at Caesar's Palace was used anyway. I got a key. I was in the bed every night."

Flynn colored. "What a nice idea," he said.

"So," she shrugged. "You fooled me. You've interviewed people who came here from Ada, Texas?"

"Some of them."

He left his room key on the desk and picked up his bag.

"Where are you going now?" she asked.

"To the airport."

"You're just wasting my time, Flynn. You think I can't find out where you're going?"

"I think you can," said Flynn. "The truth is I myself don't know where I'm going. I hope to make up my mind on the flight to Chicago." He grinned at her. "Fact is, I hate bein' observed when I don't know what I'm doin'."

"I see."

"I don't understand this situation much better than when I started in on it. And, as the man says, time's a-wastin'."

"Oh, all right. You're known for playing close to your chest, but this is ridiculous. Listen, Flynn, I know you're not responsible to the great G. of the U.S., but, dammit, I am. The letter of introduction I showed you wasn't signed by a county attorney, you know."

"It wasn't signed at all."

"It was handwritten!" she whispered loudly. "By the President of the United States!"

"An impressive fellow," said Flynn. "Scrupulous about his appearance in public. You'll never catch that fellow in a dirty shirt."

"What are you talking about?"

"Coming to the airport with me?"

"My luggage is in your room at Caesar's Palace."

"Ach, that's right," said Flynn. "Check out for me, will you? I keep forgetting that little particular."

14

"Honestly, Frannie," Elizabeth said as she settled down to Sunday family dinner at her end of the table. "You have no idea how much things cost."

"I do," said Flynn. "I just paid a hotel bill in Las Vegas."

"Las Vegas!" said Todd, one of the twin fifteen-year-old sons. "Were you in Las Vegas?"

"Gamboling on the green," muttered Winny, trying his salad.

On the flight to Chicago, Flynn had been unable to make up his mind whether to go to Washington immediately (as the assault on the Pentagon Intelligence section seemed to worry everyone the most), directly to Cleary's Mountain, Cleary, Oregon, to interview the pig woman's son, George Udine, or to begin arranging a trip to Solensk, U.S.S.R., to interview Cecil Hill, renowned counterfeiter.

Something told Flynn he should stop in at East Frampton next, but maybe that was only because he had first heard of East Frampton in this case immediately after hearing of Ada. No, it was more than that: without spending much time on it he had to establish the two towns either had something in common, or they didn't.

Nodding over his Lipton tea on the airplane (when would airlines begin serving herb teas?), Flynn considered that the unexpected largesse had caused almost everyone to leave Ada, Texas, except the minister; apparently it had caused almost no one to leave East Frampton, Massachusetts, except two members of the clergy, the Congregational minister, who had gone to tour Europe, and the Catholic priest, who had gone to join the missionaries. Was that significant? Flynn smiled at the thought. He was swatting fleas.

As N.N. Zero guessed he would, Flynn decided to go home. He arrived late Saturday in time to collect the twins from a school dance, see all his five children in their beds, and have a long sleep himself.

Flynn sat down to his Sunday roast beef with his family.

Around the dining-room table, to his right, were Randy and Todd, the twins; to his left, twelve-year-old Jenny with her blue saucer eyes, and, next to his mother, nine-year-old Winny. Baby Jeff had been fed his bottle and placed upstairs to play with his toes.

The children had been full of their news.

"Honestly," Elizabeth fussed, "we're now paying more for a simple head of lettuce or a pound of peas than we used to spend for an entire dinner for the family. Don't ask what this roast beef cost."

"I won't," agreed Flynn.

"Shoes!" Elizabeth exclaimed.

"It's the money they spend on advertising," Flynn said, "notifying us how cheap everything is, that makes everything so expensive."

"Toothpaste!" expostulated Elizabeth.

Flynn remembered that as a boy, in the last days of the Third Reich, he had learned to clean his teeth with mud, rinsing them with ditch water. Mud was still cheap.

And all his children had sparkling teeth.

"Some brokerage house," Elizabeth said, helping the unwilling Winny to the broccoli, "has been keeping what they call a Trivia Index. Instead of recording the rate of inflation of those things on the Consumers' Price Index kept by the government, for food, fuel, shelter, whatever else, they've kept track of the rate of inflation on things that aren't essential but we all buy—like ice cream cones and brooms. And you know, they've discovered the rate of inflation on these items is nothing like what we believe, having only the Consumers' Index to go on. They say the inflation rate on these items is as much as five and six hundred percent!"

"Sure," said Flynn, remembering the insanity he had just seen in Las Vegas, hands throwing "cash money" on a table and other hands picking the "cash money" up from the table as fast as hands could move, with neither goods nor services changing hands at all, "and the people are throwing away their money on trivia faster than ever before because the money means less to them than it did yesterday and they suspect it will mean even less tomorrow."

He was rather glad the broccoli had not been passed down to his end of the table.

"What causes inflation?" Jenny asked her father.

"Ask your mother."

She had survived wild inflation in Israel and other places before they were married.

"Too much money," Elizabeth said.

"Then why don't they stop making money?"

"Because it keeps people employed."

"Then what's wrong with inflation?"

"Because the more money there is the less value it has and even the employed people become poorer and poorer."

Flynn smiled at his wife. She could fit the history of the world into a thimble without threat of overflow. He had no doubt she was a direct descendant of the person—probably a woman—who had written Genesis, or at least edited it.

He had no idea whether she was right about the economic forces at play in the world, but he noticed the children looked pleasantly informed.

"Everyone from the Boston Police has called to see how you are, Frannie," Elizabeth said. "Commissioner D'Esopo. The mayor's called. Grover's called at least every other day. He's been most solicitous."

"I suppose Grover himself suffers good health?"

"I guess so."

"Drat," said Flynn.

Flynn had spent much effort trying to get his assistant, Grover, out from under him.

"The blithering idiot," said Flynn. "How am I, anyway, now that I ask?"

"Recovering nicely," answered his wife.

"Oh? And from what am I recovering this time?"

"Appendicitis."

"The operation was successful, was it? The patient survived?"

"You're doing as well as can be expected," Elizabeth said.

"Didn't I have appendicitis last year," Flynn asked, "over that other matter in Chad?"

"You can't have appendicitis more than once, Da," said Randy.

"Precisely."

Elizabeth said, "Colitis. You had colitis last year."

"Ah, yes," said Flynn. "I'm glad you keep my medical records for me, Elsbeth. Otherwise I wouldn't have a clue what to say when people ask me how I am."

"You're as well as can be expected," Elizabeth said.

"I'm not done with this N.N. matter, you know," Flynn said, "just because I'm home for the day. You'll have to make up more excuses for my absence from the Boston Police Department."

Elizabeth shrugged. "I guess you'll have complications."

"That's the truth," Flynn said. "Complications I have."

Winny said, "Da didn't get any broccoli."

"Oh, my," said Flynn in mock dismay. "I was never passed the broccoli."

"Pass your father the broccoli, Winny," Elizabeth said.

The little scamp was already doing so, his eyes alight.

Flynn felt the bowl with the palm of his hand.

"Wouldn't it be cold now?"

"I'll heat it up," Elizabeth said.

"Never mind."

Taking care not to look at Winny, Flynn spooned some broccoli, a very little, onto the edge of his plate.

"Funny," Elizabeth said. "Cocky only called once to ask how you are."

"Cocky knows how I am, I suspect," said Flynn. "He has three-quarters of the brains of the Boston Police Department between his own ears."

Detective Lieutenant Walter Concannon (retired handicapped) unofficially worked with Flynn, and invariably beat him at chess. He knew Flynn, well.

"He asked if you were so stopped by the Knibridge Gambit you wouldn't come to the office," Elizabeth said.

"Knibridge? He couldn't have said Knibridge Gambit," Flynn said. "I never heard of the Knibridge Gambit."

"Maybe that's why you're stumped by it," Todd said.

"Maybe . . ."

"Are you going back to Las Vegas?" Elizabeth asked.

"No."

"At least you can't starve in Las Vegas," Winny said.

"I'm going someplace," Flynn said, hesitantly.

Elizabeth's look asked him if he wanted more questions.

"So what's the answer to the riddle you gave me?" Randy asked.

"What riddle?"

"On the phone. What can depopulate a town in Texas, drive the people of a town in Massachusetts crazy, and wrack up the Pentagon?"

"Oh," Flynn said. "That riddle."

"What's the answer?" said Jenny.

"I said a skunk," said Randy.

"Mrs. Williams," said Todd. "She could do all that."

"Who's Mrs. Williams?" asked Flynn.

"Our math teacher."

"Oh," said Flynn.

After dinner they would all repair to the living room, to the piano and stringed instruments, and have their little musicale. Flynn had not been informed what piece the youngsters had been practicing to play with him that day. Flynn looked forward to that. It would give him a chance to think.

"You can't starve to death in Las Vegas," Winny insisted.

"The areas are so unlike each other," Elizabeth said. "I think. Massachusetts, Texas, D.C. I mean, I was thinking of a mineral seepage, or something, you know. . . ."

Flynn did not know and would not ask. He was not at the point where he wanted this particular problem thimblized.

"So what's the answer?" asked Jenny.

"The root of all evil," said Flynn.

"Money?" Randy said.

"Money?" Jenny said.

"At least," Winny said, "you cannot starve in Las Vegas."

Flynn said: "Money. Apparently every citizen of Ada, Texas, every citizen of East Frampton, Massachusetts, every member of a Pentagon Intelligence section woke up one fine day—or, I should say, three different fine days—and discovered they each—every man, woman, and child—had been given anonymously, and apparently without reason, one hundred thousand dollars in cash."

"Wick!" said Randy.

"Ex!" said Todd.

"Apparent results," said Flynn: "the people of one town ran away; the people of another town kept everyone else away; the people working in the Pentagon grew distinctly shiftless."

"East Frampton," Elizabeth said. "We went out there two summers ago."

"I don't think that had anything to do with it," Flynn said.

Winny said, "I knew we should have stayed longer."

"That's some riddle," Randy said.

"The riddle," Flynn said, "is who and why."

"Who gave the money and why?" Elizabeth, watched by ten eyes, was cutting a chocolate layer cake.

"So what's the answer?" Jenny said.

"Get away with you," Flynn said. "Why do I come home at all? All the help I get from this collection of ravenous nincompoops."

"Da didn't finish his broccoli," Winny observed. He was clearing away the plates.

Flynn said, "It was cold."

"I could have heated it," Elizabeth said.

"It was too late in the meal when I got it," Flynn said.

Winny said, "Da doesn't like broccoli. Either."

"Clear the table, Winny. Here, you others, help Winny clear the table before I serve the cake."

The children clattered back and forth to the kitchen.

Over the cake, Elizabeth said, "That's a great deal of money, Frannie."

"A dreadful lot."

"Well," she said. "I'm sure the answer's very simple."

"You're always sure the answer's very simple."

"And have I ever been wrong?" she asked.

"Not yet," begrudged Flynn.

"Da *likes* chocolate cake!" announced Winny, stuffing his own mouth.

"Now," Flynn said, "I have a very important question."

They all looked at him apprehensively.

"For Winny."

They all looked relieved, except Winny, who continued to look apprehensive.

"Winny," Flynn said slowly. "Answer me this . . . if you can. I know you're not ready for the question . . . the topic is new to you, and all . . ." Winny swallowed his cake in a gulp and stared at his father. "Winny . . . why can't you starve to death in Las Vegas?"

After Jenny giggled and the boys snickered, Winny, with a straight face, still staring at his father, said, "What?"

"Why . . . can't you starve to death in Las Vegas?"

"I didn't get the question, sir."

"The question," Flynn said with mock patience, "is why can't one starve in Las Vegas?"

"Why can't one starve in Las Vegas?" Winny asked blankly.

"That's the question," Flynn said. "What's the answer?"

"Oh, what's the answer, Winny?" Giggling, Jenny punched him on the arm.

Winny shrugged. "Because of the sand which is there."

Without cracking a smile, he returned to his chocolate layer cake.

15

In his stout shoes, tweed suit, and raincoat, Flynn was pleased to remain on the sunny, windy deck of the converted dragger as it moved slowly out of the harbor.

As the ferry was passing the entrance buoy, she picked up speed and began a nice canter over the low swells.

The wizened deck man who had been coiling the lines slowly, now went up to the deckhouse and took the wheel.

The captain of the ferry, a lean man of about twenty, came down to the deck near Flynn and re-settled the lines. He gave Flynn a friendly nod.

Flynn was the only passenger.

Also on deck were stacked crates of whiskey, gin, soda water, backgammon, and electrical appliances all marked for East Frampton delivery.

Over the wind, Flynn shouted, "Someone in East Frampton planning a party?"

The captain grinned. "East Frampton is a party. They been a party all summer and fall. Longest happy hour I ever see."

"What do you mean?"

"Didn't you read about those people chasin' the tourists out of town beginning of summer?"

"I heard something about it."

The skipper said, "Damnedest thing ever."

"What caused the riot?"

Hands in the pockets of his thick jacket, the young skipper shrugged. "Got me. Somethin' weird's been goin' on in that little corner of the universe. All summer long." The young skipper bounced the toe of his sneaker against the side of a crate a few times. "You know the island?"

"Not very well. I've been there once before, for the day."

"Ride in the car—you see about everything in a half-hour. Walk on the beach. The movie show's open only Friday, Saturday in the winter."

"Pretty lively place."

"I used to know a girl over there—never mind her name. We dated a few times, last winter. As much of a date as you can have on the island. Tried to get her to come over to the mainland with me, but she never would come. Well, she'd come over to look at the stores and have a sandwich for the day and come back on the ferry. Everyone did that. What I mean is"
—the young man seemed to be concentrating on the toe of his sneaker—"I couldn't get her to come over for the night."

He looked at Flynn.

Flynn smiled at him.

"She was really looking forward to comin' over to Boston this year, to go to school. She wanted to be a nurse. She'd been accepted and everything. She'd been working in the drugstore since she was fifteen, saving money."

Spray came over the bow and landed at their feet.

"All of a sudden . . . well, I don't know. I went over to see her one day. This was just after the riot. She had no time for me. She was there at the house, with her brother. She had fancy new clothes. We were in the kitchen. Her brother was drinkin' beer. They kept lookin' at each other and winkin' and laughin'. They never did let me in on what was so funny. He kept sayin' things like, 'Maybe I'll buy a Corvette. Maybe I'll buy a Porsche.' And she'd go, 'Maybe we'll go halves and buy a Rolls.' This kid, her brother, did lousy in school. Mostly he worked in the fish house. Well, he wasn't workin' in the fish house that Tuesday. And he did buy a fancy car—a Datsun 280-Z. I saw him with it in Frampton a few weeks later. She was with him, laughin', hair blowin' in the wind. Neither one of them saw me." The young man averted his head slightly and looked across the sea. "I think somethin' funny's goin' on between her and her brother. There's a nasty word for it."

Flynn waited a moment, for the charge to evaporate in the air.

"She never did come over to the mainland for school, eh?"

The young skipper shook his head, "No." He laughed. "One day, in September, I stopped in East Frampton, and was just walkin' down their shoppin' street. This guy—he's been on this ferry a hundred times—stops me in the street and just says, 'Get outta here, Tom.' "

"Did you get?"

"Sure. Who cares?"

"So what's going on in that small corner of the universe?" Flynn asked.

"I don't know. The F.B.I. man from New Bedford's been down a half a dozen times. I've talked to him, just like I'm talkin' to you. He admits the people in East Frampton have a lot of money, now. At least, they're spendin' a lot of money. No one's workin' for a livin' over there. East Frampton's three draggers didn't go out all summer. The fish house is closed. I've talked to the coast guard guys, too."

"What do you think happened?" Flynn asked.

"Your guess is as good as mine."

"No, it's not."

The young captain smiled at him. "Well, we all know the drug ships from South America have been comin' farther north the last few years."

"Have you ever seen 'em yourself?"

"Well, I've seen some small ships, not built for these waters, flying foreign flags hangin' around out here, seemin' to go nowhere."

"Doesn't the coast guard see them?"

"They pick one up once in a while. The coast guard watches 'em to try and see where they're goin'. But they never seem to be goin' anywhere. If a cutter goes for them on the open sea, you can see little splashes off the freighter's stern. If you get my drift."

"So you think East Frampton's the place the stuff finally comes ashore."

The young skipper said, "It's my best guess."

"Sure, a whole town wouldn't give in to such a thing. Smugglin' drugs."

"There's a lot of money in it," the captain said. "A lot of muscle behind it, I suspect."

"But a whole town," said Flynn. "Conspirin' . . ."

"My granddad tells me that during Prohibition—you know, back in the twenties?—liquor used to come ashore here."

"East Frampton?"

"East Frampton and lots of places."

"There's a difference, lad. Rum's one thing, heroin's another."

The skipper said, "They're both drugs."

"That they are, lad. That they are."

"You with the F.B.I.?"

"Is that why you're talkin' with me?"

"Well, you're not a tourist this time of year. And you don't look like a businessman."

"And why don't I?"

"You're too . . . burly."

"Burly, is it? There's a word and a half."

"You haven't spent your life sittin' in an office—any more'n I intend to."

"Not much of it, anyway."

"So are you?"

"F.B.I.? No, I'm not."

"You're mighty interested in East Frampton."

"You noticed the gentle questionin', did you?"

"Well, I don't know who you are, but I don't mind tellin' you what I think about East Frampton. The place has gone nuts."

"And you think it's drug smugglin' they're into."

"Yeah."

"But I gather from what you know, talkin' to the F.B.I. man and the coast guard, they can't find any evidence of such a thing."

"I guess not."

"But it's your opinion suddenly everyone in East Frampton has a lot of money."

"Two things," the young skipper said. "First is: they have a lot of money. Second is: the people in that town want to keep everyone else away from them." He frowned. "To the point where a girl I thought I liked . . . I think has gone to incest."

"Ah," said Flynn. "And that's always the part that hurts. The human part."

The entrance to Frampton Harbor wasn't far off the bow.

"Are you going to return to the mainland tonight?"

"Yes," said Flynn. "I expect so."

"We pull out at four-thirty sharp," the young skipper said. "Whoever you are, it's real important you do whatever you can for the people of that crazy town. They've got a bad case of degeneracy, I'd say."

16

"How do I get service?" Flynn finally asked in his mildest voice.

He had taxied to East Frampton. (The old driver had said, "My sister-in-law lives over here"—he even pointed out the little white house as they passed it—"seventy-two years old and gone cranky. Wife can't even talk to her on the phone anymore. Always spends Christmas with us, but doubt she will this year. Funny what happens to people sometimes. Never saw anyone who acts so much like the cat who swallowed the parakeet.") Flynn had ambled up and down Reardon Street, six blocks long, curved around the narrow harbor. The souvenir and clothing shops, and the one or two good restaurants were closed, for the winter. So were the grocery store, hardware store, and drug store. Flynn stared at the restaurant where he had taken his family two summers before. The baked, stuffed lobster had been delicious. Now the restaurant's sign was lopsided, hanging by a single nail. The window near the main door was smashed. Back down Reardon Street, near the center of East Frampton, the grass around the Congregational church looked as if it had not been cut all summer. The church's signboard said, JOY! HE IS RISEN!, which Flynn guessed had been the message since Easter. No one answered the door at the parish house. He could not find anything identified as the priest's house in the vicinity of the Catholic church. The sign on the door of the police station said, OUT TO LUNCH with the word *lunch* crossed out and the words LYNCH FOREIGNERS written in. The door was locked. The few people in the street had stared through him from a distance. The one or two he began to approach crossed the street to avoid him. "Sure," said Flynn to himself. "And didn't I take a shower this morning?"

He had also walked up and down the beach near the town, studying the harbor, which could be better described as a long, narrow inlet, and inspecting the town wharf. No one was on the wharf. The one fishing boat docked against it (two others rode at moorings in the harbor) was low in the water. Bilge water must be skirting her engines.

The only place in town he could find open was a bar-restaurant, low-ceilinged, dark, with hewn wooden beams. The floor was filthy.

Two groups of men were sitting in back booths, drinking beer and playing backgammon. They ignored Flynn when he entered.

A jukebox was playing music with a heavy, thumping beat.

Again Flynn said, "How do I get service?"

A fat man at the edge of one of the booths said, "What do you want?"

"I was thinking a shrimp salad sandwich and a glass of milk?"

"You got two hundred dollars?" the man said.

"What for?"

"A shrimp salad sandwich and a glass of milk."

"Costs that much, does it?"

"It ain't worth my time to move for less."

There was low laughter from the booths.

Flynn rose and walked slowly over to the booths.

The men's jocosity left them as they stared up at Flynn's full chest and shoulders, which appeared even bigger in comparison to his small head.

"Season's over, mister," said the fat man.

"Yeah," said a younger man sitting nearest the wall. "Come back in four or five years."

"Or never," muttered another man.

"Well, now," said Flynn. "You haven't asked me the exact nature of my business."

"Not open for business," said the fat man.

The younger man said, "What business?"

"If it hasn't to do with backgammon," a toothless old man said, "we're not interested."

The only man in the booths wearing a necktie said, "You're not the scout, are you? From the Paradise Island Backgammon Tournament? We sent in applications."

Flynn said, in honesty, "My name's Flynn. . . ."

"You're Mister Flynn?" said the necktie.

The men looked at him with new interest.

"Yes," said Flynn. "I am Flynn."

"Someone was here looking for you," the young man said. "Yesterday. She asked all over town for you."

"Oh?"

"The most beautiful girl in the world," the young man said. "Weird eyes, though."

"The cockeyed beauty," said the toothless one.

"Said her name was Ducey Webb. She was sure you were here, or had been here. But she made a big mystery out of what you'd be doing here."

"Should have guessed you're the scout for Paradise Island," asserted a whiskey-soaked voice.

The man in the necktie stood up, which wasn't all that easy, as he had been in a middle seat of the booth. "Will you play backgammon with us, Mister Flynn? Manny is the undisputed town champion." He indicated the man across the table from him.

Manny was a thirty-year-old, cow-eyed fisherman whose face seemed incapable of expression.

"Well, now," said Flynn. "I wouldn't mind watching while the game is being played. . . ."

"Who should play for you?" asked the necktie.

"Why, the number-one and number-two player, seeing you've ranked yourselves so formally." Flynn sat on the seat at the edge of the booth vacated for him by the fat man. "You've been running tournaments yourselves, have you?"

"That's all they ever do," said the toothless one.

"However," said Flynn, "seeing you asked, I do admit to being a trifle hungry. . . ."

"Anything you want, Mister Flynn," said the fat man. "Whiskey?"

"Ach, no." The man in the necktie—apparently the number-two player—sat down again. He and Manny were busy arranging the board for a new game. "I must keep my head clear to observe the play."

"A beer?"

"Oddly enough," said Flynn, "my mind was runnin' more toward a shrimp salad sandwich and a glass of milk. Is such a thing possible, do you suppose?"

"Anything you want," said the fat man.

"And for a price marginally less than two hundred dollars, I would hope?"

"We can afford to buy you lunch, Mister Flynn." Chuckling, the fat man went into the kitchen area.

"You came all the way up here from Paradise Island," observed the youngest man. "We only sent in the applications two weeks ago."

Flynn neither confirmed nor denied. He observed the superstructure of lies people build for themselves.

"How did you hear"—the toothless man spoke slowly—"this town has developed some pretty good backgammon players?"

"Word gets around," said Flynn. "It travels slowly but, sooner or later, it gets around. My, my. The things I've heard about East Frampton, Massachusetts."

A shrimp salad sandwich, a bowl of clam chowder, and a tall glass of milk were placed in front of him.

"Now that's what I call bein' out to lunch," said Flynn.

He did not insult his hosts by hesitating to eat.

Even though the dice were thrown, the whiskey-voiced man, staring at Flynn, said, "What else have you heard about this town?"

"Well . . ." Flynn had three spoonfuls of chowder, "I've heard that during Prohibition more rum passed through East Frampton in the dark of the night than has even yet passed through the bellies of the whole Cuban government."

"True," grinned the toothless man. "I was in charge of samplin' it, before the rest of it was sent to the mainland."

The men resumed their game.

Flynn had five spoonfuls of chowder. "I hear the ships carrying drugs from Latin America are now coming up into these waters."

Most of the men were watching the game with obsessive interest.

It was a moment before the men listening to Flynn realized what he meant.

The man with the whiskey voice answered him with narrow eyes. "Listen, mister: anyone who tries to land any of that stuff in East Frampton is going to get himself filleted and thrown back into the sea."

Flynn considered the image while he chewed his sandwich, and watched the game.

He knew very little about backgammon. Once, on a long, boring train trip through Rumania, he had read a book about the game by Alexis Obolensky. Flynn never played it.

Flynn's life, at its happiest, included a running game of chess with Lieutenant Walter (Cocky) Concannon. Games of chance did not make him happy.

He pretended to put a professional eye on the game, being sure not to commit himself to an opinion by either facial or verbal expression.

The two men played with baffling speed. They passed the dice back and forth, threw them, and adjusted the backgammon men on the board almost faster than the eye could track.

Flynn felt a wholly irrelevant theory nudging his mind. It had something to do with the obsessive behavior adopted by some people who enjoy financial freedom. He'd have to leave that speculation until after he retired.

Necktie's eyes darted about the board. Manny's eyes saw everything without appearing to move.

Knowing little about the game, Flynn soon concluded Manny would be the winner.

"Tell me," Flynn said, "just to keep up the chatter and distract the players, mind you—not many tournaments enjoy the luxury of such silence—doesn't George Udine have something to do with East Frampton?"

"Who?" said a voice absently.

"George Udine. Of the Udine Corporation. Maybe you know him better as George Lewis."

"No."

"Yeah," said the youngest man. "He came by a couple of summers ago."

"He did," confirmed another.

"He did?" Flynn said by way of encouragement.

"In this humungous yacht," the youngest man said. "Barely fit in the harbor. Had to anchor way out."

"Never came ashore," said the toothless one.

"He had a senator and an actress on board," said the youngest man. "They came ashore."

"But Udine himself never came ashore, is that it?" Flynn asked lazily.

"They were only here overnight," said the youngest.

Flynn finished his chowder, his sandwich, and his

milk. He waited for the game to get into its final stages before springing his big question—in his own way.

" 'Course, I also heard what happened to this town last spring. April, was it?"

Again, only a few of the obsessed men gave him a quick glance.

"Now, that was a remarkable thing," Flynn said.

Others gave him a quick glance, but no one said anything.

"Just think of it," Flynn said.

There was no answer.

"That such a thing should happen to a town."

No answer.

"Every man, woman, and child of you."

No answer.

Flynn glanced around and saw faces reddening and jaws tightening. It seemed to him the action on the backgammon board had slowed. Their obsession with the game had diminished.

"Marvelous thing, that," mused Flynn.

No answer. But three were sitting back staring at him.

"Every man, woman, and child of you waking up one fine day and finding one hundred thousand dollars in cash in your laps."

The game stopped.

Everyone, including the players, was watching Flynn.

He was glad he had eaten.

Flynn said, mildly, "Hell of a place to leave the game. Do you mean to declare a winner at this point?"

The man in the necktie said, "What are you talking about, mister?"

"Backgammon," asserted Flynn.

After a long pause, the man in the necktie said, "You said something about everyone in this town receiving some money last spring."

"Ach, sure," said Flynn. "Everyone knows that."

"What do you mean, 'everyone knows that,'" said whiskey voice.

"Didn't I read about it in the *Wall Street Journal*?" said Flynn. "Or was it about some other town?" He looked from staring face to staring face. Pulses throbbed in their temples. "Ach, no. I'm sure it said East Frampton, Massachusetts."

Two men in the booth behind Flynn got up and left the building.

The man with the necktie said, "What do you want, mister?"

Flynn said, "As long as I know about this remarkable occurrence, whatever the source of my knowledge, I'd like to ask you gentlemen—quietly, mind you—your opinion as to where such scads of money came from . . . ?"

More men left the room.

Beside Flynn, Manny got up and indicated he wanted to get out of the booth.

"A simple question . . ." said Flynn.

Manny stepped over him.

A steady stream of men made for the door.

Finally only the man in the necktie remained seated, staring at Flynn across the table.

"Surely," Flynn said directly to the man in the necktie, "in all this time you must have wondered where the money came from . . . ?"

The man in the necktie stood up. He said, "Whatever you're talkin' about, mister, it didn't happen."

"What didn't happen?" asked Flynn.

"You know what didn't happen," the man said.

17

He had arranged for the taxi to return to East Frampton to pick him up in front of the drugstore at three o'clock.

He found himself waiting at a quarter to two.

The street was empty. It had been empty since he came out of the restaurant. How the men who had been in the restaurant with him had disappeared that fast was a puzzle. There had been only one car, a Jaguar XKE, parked in front of the restaurant. Every other building on the street was closed. Every neighborhood has its nooks and crannies known only to its denizens. He wondered if they were peeking around corners at him.

"Sure, I'm about as popular," Flynn muttered to himself, "as a skin doctor with a rash."

He looked up and down the street for a place to sit. There was none. "An uncivil town," he noted to himself. "Must remember to send Grover here, first chance I get."

The sun was bright. At two-twenty there was no longer shade on the Reardon Street side of the drugstore. Flynn went to the corner and peered around it.

There, in the shade, his back and one sneakered foot leaning against the brick wall, hands folded across his chest, was a teenaged boy.

"Hallo," said Flynn cheerily. "I was looking for you."

The boy looked at Flynn suspiciously. "Me?"

"You."

The boy spat through his teeth. "What do you want?"

"I want to know why a likely lad such as yourself, with his whole life ahead of him, is standing around this dead town."

Again the boy spat through his teeth. "What's a 'likely lad'?"

"You are," said Flynn, trying his best to sound convincing.

"You think I should leave this burg?"

Flynn waved at the town around him. "The place isn't bustlin' with opportunity now, is it?"

"Not much goin' on," agreed the boy. "Unless you're a backgammon nut."

"You don't like backgammon?"

"I don't get to play. No money."

"What happened to your money?" Flynn asked. The boy searched his face. "Don't worry, lad. I know about the money. Last April you were given one hundred thousand dollars. What happened to it?"

"My father took it. Even though my name was on it. He says it's his. I'm seventeen. A minor, he says."

"And what do you say?"

"I say my name was on it. Every other kid in town got money. At least got to buy a car, or somethin'."

"Did every man, woman, and child in this town get one hundred thousand dollars last April?" Flynn asked innocently. The kid spat again. A face of spit was beginning to appear on the sidewalk. "You can tell me, lad. Apparently you have nothing to lose."

"Sure . . ." said the kid. "Everybody."

"Where did the money come from?"

"It was dumped outside everybody's house. One morning it was just there. In big brown envelopes." He grinned. "One guy didn't get his."

"Oh?"

"Lived upstairs in a two-family house. Slept late. Drunk the night before." He spat and a left ear appeared on the face. "Heard everybody else in town got money. Figured his downstairs neighbor took his. So he shot him." The kid laughed.

"Shot him dead?"

The kid nodded yes.

"And had the neighbor stolen the money?"

"It was in his refrigerator."

"Fat lot of good the money did him, though," asserted Flynn. "Arrested. Tried. Imprisoned."

"He was never arrested." The boy turned his head sideways and spat and a mouth appeared on the face. "You think everyone in town is going to risk losing one hundred big ones just to see one more punk in jail? No way." Squinting, the boy looked up and down the street. "This has become a real quiet town, mister. Keeps a lot of things quiet, nowadays. They've all gone nuts. Everybody in town. They all hide behind their doors afraid some turkey like you is going to show up and tell them all to give the money back. 'Fraid of bein' robbed. There's been more than one shooting in this town lately, I can tell you. More like a dozen."

Quietly, Flynn said, "And you've no idea who did this to the town?"

The boy shook his head. "Who cares? Some nut. Some nut just decided to drop a whole lot of money on the town to drive the whole town nuts. And he succeeded."

"What about yourself?" Flynn asked.

"I'm just waitin' until I'm eighteen."

"What then? Join the navy?"

"Nope." The boy spat a nose onto the sidewalk. The face was complete.

"What are you going to do?"

"Depends." Again the boy looked out into the sunlight. "If my father doesn't let me have my money then, I'll kill him. Then maybe I'll leave town. Maybe I won't." He stood up from the wall, dropped his arms, and started ambling loose-jointed up the sidewalk. "I'm not joinin' no navy."

At the back corner of the drugstore, the boy turned around and walked a few steps backward. "You oughta get outta town now, though, mister." He wasn't speaking very loudly. "So many skeletons at the bottom of the harbor now, one more won't matter."

Flynn watched him cross the side street, go into a vacant lot, and disappear behind a huge pile of rubbish.

The taxi arrived at ten minutes past three.

18

Landing in Washington, D.C., that night, Flynn mused at all the years of effort N.N. had expended to keep Francis Xavier Flynn away from Washington (and London and Paris and Bonn and Rome and other national capitals); away from nationalistically motivated governmental committees who wanted to know more of how the international, private, between-the-borders organization N.N. operated, and a great deal more of Flynn's personal biography.

Flynn's death had been reported, convincingly, a dozen times. He had been put "on ice," under his own name, as an inspector (*the* inspector) of the Boston Police Department. But N.N. Zero continued to wheel him out when the need arose, and ride him through one more extraordinary (always "extraordinary") case. Last year when Flynn was in Chad, the Boston Police were told that he had colitis. This year, on this case, appendicitis. There was no one more robust than Flynn.

Crossing from the airplane to the terminal, Flynn wondered what he'd die of at the end of this case.

* * *

The hotel desk clerk looked puzzled at Flynn.

"You're already checked in, sir."

"Am I, indeed?"

The clerk pulled a registration card from the file and looked at it, then compared it with the one Flynn had just filled out, looked even more puzzled, and handed both cards to Flynn.

They were identical—to the home address given, credit-card number, even signature.

"My, my," said Flynn.

He handed the cards back to the clerk.

"One of those cards should be destroyed."

"Of course." The clerk tore one of the registration cards in quarters, as if its existence were an embarrassment to everyone.

"Do you feel all right, sir?"

"I do. Yes, I do."

"There is a doctor we could summon. The hotel guests find him quite satisfactory . . . and, er, discreet."

"I'm very well," said Flynn.

"It must have been just a lapse of memory."

"Something of the sort," said Flynn.

"Do you have them often, sir?"

"What?"

"Lapses of memory. Did you forget the question?"

"No, I did not forget the question—I'm amazed at it. And no, I've never had a lapse of memory in my life, to my continuous regret."

"I have an old aunt who has lapses of memory. Of course, she is eighty-nine. She comes and goes, comes and goes."

"Like a certain poet, from St. Louis, Mo.," muttered Flynn.

"Sir?"

"I need to know my room number!"

"Ah, yes." The clerk's smile was superior. "Of course, I wasn't on duty when you checked in the first time, at four o'clock this afternoon. . . ."

"The room number . . ."

"Eleven twenty-three."

"And I need the key!"

"But, sir . . ."

"The key, dammit!"

The clerk held the key to Room 1123 in his hand. "I'll call the bellman. —Front!"

Flynn took the key from the desk clerk's hand.

"I don't need the bellman," Flynn said. "I've already checked in. Don't you remember? I'll carry my own bag!"

In Room 1123 Ducey Webb, naked, was curled in a chair, reading *Cosmopolitan* magazine.

"Oh, hullo, Flynn."

" 'Hullo,' is it?" He lowered his suitcase to the floor and closed the hotel-room door. "Seldom have I had such an open greeting."

She dropped the magazine. Her blue and brown eyes watched him watch her. Leisurely she stretched her whole body in the chair. Ducey Webb's physical perfection provided her perfect poise while perfectly naked.

"Thanks for checking me in," Flynn said. "It's a service I didn't know I needed."

"It's something I learned to do," she said, imitating the rhythm of his speech, "checking you out of Caesar's Palace, in Las Vegas. Are you chastened?"

"Chased is more like it."

"I've been looking for you high and low."

"You should have just looked low," said Flynn, "as that's where I've been."

She stood up, picked up his suitcase, and swung it onto the double bed.

"What do you think you're doing?"

She was unpacking him.

"If you think I need to play house with a slip of a girl—or, a girl without a slip, if I may so amend myself—"

"Oh, shut up, Francis."

"—a girl young enough to be of more interest to my sons than the ordinary football—"

"How old are you anyway, Flynn?"

"I'm pushin' forty," said Flynn. "From the north side."

"Oh, come on." Beginning to unpack him, she loosened his necktie. "You can't tell me you have no more interest in me than in a football."

"Well," said Flynn. "You're about the same color."

She put his hand on her hip. "A little smoother, wouldn't you say?"

"Aye, that. But I have the suspicion your bounce is just as tricky."

She put her hand behind her neck and turned slowly in the air. There were mirrors everywhere in the room, and Ducey was in each.

"Not the same shape at all, Flynn."

"I admit: you're something I hate to pass. . . ."

From the distance of two meters her eyes locked on his. "But you're going to, aren't you, Flynn? Instead of making love with me, you're going to make jokes?"

He gulped. "I am."

"What's in your head, Flynn?"

"Suspicions. Wee voices of warning in the back of the cranium."

"Of what, for God's sake?"

"You have to admit, Ms. Webb, your approach has been odd."

"Odd?" She wrinkled her face at him.

"Marked by a combination of the ingenuous and the disingenuous."

"What?"

"The direct and the indirect."

"I understand English." She shook her head. "No one understands the Irish."

"You followed me in a yellow Fiat convertible from Austin, Texas. Yet after following me awhile, you suddenly turn off down a dirt road. You could have caught up to me—that is, if it was your purpose to work with me."

The skin over her cheekbones darkened. "I wanted to change clothes. Into something cooler."

"You raised a lot of dust and wasted considerable gasoline giving vent to your modesty."

"There's a difference between the eyes of Texas and smiling, Irish eyes."

"Is there? I'd say it's more likely that at that point of the trip you were able to confirm I was definitely headed for Ada, Texas."

"Confirm to whom? How?"

"Next you pop into Bob's Diner with two extraordinary things. The first was a letter of introduction handwritten by the President of the United States, no less, unsigned, as if it were from the bowers of the imperial bedchamber."

"Have you checked its authenticity?"

"No."

She placed her hand on her hip.

"The second wondrous thing you brought to our meeting at Bob's Diner is woolly speculation regarding Ada itself: that there could be vast quantities of oil underneath; that the town could be schemed for a radioactive-materials dump."

"What's wrong with that?"

"With your own apparent resources you could have checked out both elements in the time it takes a wee lamb to give the world a steady gaze and say, 'Baa!' "

She sat in the chair.

"Next you pop up in my bed in Las Vegas, my investigation in East Frampton, and now, very much in my view, here in Washington."

She fitted a toe against the faded pattern of the rug.

"I'm just trying to help."

"I'll repeat, in my own way: your help seems both oddly personal and oddly distracting."

"Well . . . we're traveling together."

"We are not traveling together."

"Flynn. I know something of your background. I know you must lead a guarded life. I know you have to be suspicious of everyone and everything, just to survive. But tell me, you big lummox: with all this darting around under bushes you've had to do, when was the last time anyone told you you are a beautiful, gorgeous man?"

"The last time someone wanted something from me. I can't figure what you want, Ms. Webb. For the life of me I can't."

"The married Flynn," she scoffed. " 'Reluctant' Flynn. I told you what I want." She gestured at her own body. "I'm concealing nothing!"

He was putting things back into his suitcase.

"Where are you going?" she asked.

"Home to Mother," he muttered.

She rose and put her arms around his neck and nuzzled his earlobe. "Flynn . . ."

"Ulysses and sirens!" exclaimed Flynn, disentangling himself. "A job's a job, for a' that. Don't you know I never mix pleasure with pleasure?"

She threw herself on the bed.

"I guess I'm insulted."

Flynn said, "I haven't the experience to know."

"Anyway," she said. "There's a message for you."

"Ach! Now we get to my business part of the business."

"A man named Sankey called. Paul Sankey. Federal Reserve Bank. Special Section. Said he'll see you at nine-thirty in the morning."

"Sankey," said Flynn.

"You're welcome," she drawled.

Ducey Webb rolled onto her side and, arm akimbo, put her head on her free hand.

"Flynn."

He snapped his suitcase shut.

"What did you learn in East Frampton?"

"Ah, there's the point," said Flynn. "You either

want my money, or what I know—and I haven't any money."

He headed for the door. "Good night to you."

"Flynn?"

Lying on the bed as she was, Ducey Webb may have been the most beautiful thing Flynn had ever seen.

She said, "I'm wet for you."

Flynn said, "Aw, dry up."

Again Flynn stood at the hotel's reception desk, suitcase in hand.

He said, rather more loudly than usual: "I'd like to check in for the night."

The desk clerk said, "Oh, no! Not again . . ."

19

According to Flynn, the city planners of Washington, D.C., were so proud of their work they weighted the entire area down with outsized architectural lumps so the city would not blow away in the winds of political fortune.

It was twenty to ten the next morning before Flynn found the right architectural lump, and five to ten before he found the Special Section, headed by Paul Sankey, within the lump, and ten past ten before Sankey had extricated himself from his staff, vaults, offices, corridors, and other machinery within the lump to join Flynn in a small lounge furnished in metal and plastic. Flynn ordered coffee and rolls for two.

Paul Sankey was a short, slim man with intense, dark eyes.

His greeting was a perfunctory nod.

He sat across the small metal table from Flynn, tipped back his chair, and crossed his arms across his chest. He ignored the coffee and roll set out before him.

Sankey said, "Eighteen years ago you and I were

together at a rather key money conference at The Hague."

"That long ago?" encouraged Flynn.

"You were young," Sankey said, "to be doing whatever you were doing. How old were you eighteen years ago?"

"Eighteen years ago? Twenty-two or twenty-three."

In fact, at that time Flynn had been so impressed by the astuteness of Paul Sankey that he considered recommending him to N.N. Ultimately he decided against it. He believed Sankey old enough to have lost the mental flexibility he would need to begin with a "between-the-borders" operation such as N.N. Eighteen years before, Sankey had been thirty-three.

Sankey said, "I never figured out what it was you were doing there. I was never sure. I'm still not sure."

"I was a guileless babe in arms," Flynn said.

"Guileless? That I've never thought. One thing I've always been sure of: somehow or other you used me."

"Used you?"

"I was manipulated somehow or other."

"Now how could that be?"

"A charming, handsome, witty young man who somehow or other got himself in and out of rooms—meetings, receptions, dinners—without ever appearing to be there, delaying someone's arrival, hastening someone's departure, putting a word in an ear here and disrupting a conversation there. You were something to watch."

"And why would you be watching me so closely?"

"Because you were young and everyone was sure you represented something significant. But no one knew what. I still don't know who or what you represented."

"Ach, sure," said Flynn. "I'm just a flatfoot at heart."

"A what?"

"A flatfoot."

Sankey's eyes swelled before looking away.

"Rightly or wrongly," Sankey said, slowly, "I have

always attributed two sentences of our ambassador's speech to you. Two key sentences. Two sentences that were not written by either him or his staff. Two sentences that he didn't know were in the speech, even as he read them. Two sentences that I have always believed you inserted in that speech somehow, the first of which was particularly significant to the world."

"Sure, now—"

"The two sentences were: 'The European Common Market will never attain an economic force equal to that of the United States of America. It is in full cognizance of this that the United States of America asures European Common Market nations of the full support of the United States of America.' "

Sankey looked accusingly at Flynn.

"Ach, well," said Flynn.

"Flynn, that statement, at that time, did more to put the whole world on the dollar standard than any other single event or statement."

"And that's bad?"

"It's ruined the economy of the world."

"I assure you I'm innocent," Flynn said, "of all the best and the worst you think of me."

"You're trying to convince me you don't understand?"

"If you can't believe in my innocence," said Flynn, "then believe in my ignorance. I have no idea what you're blatherin' about, man."

Sankey stared at him, shook his head. "You're very convincing, Flynn. You always were."

"I should be—especially when I'm tellin' the truth."

Finally Sankey smiled. "Why are you here now, Flynn?"

"A simple matter. I doubt I need the attentions of such an august personage as yourself."

"I wanted to see you anyway . . . when I heard you made a request to come in. . . . I wanted to . . ." Sankey looked off into a corner of the room, as if unable to remember what he was saying, "to see you again."

"Now that you've had the rare privilege of seein' me," said Flynn, "may I ask what the Special Section of the Federal Reserve does? I'm always eager to expand my befuddlement."

Sankey glanced at him quickly and then answered as if by rote. "We've been setting up new systems to conduct the flow of money."

"Oh," said Flynn. "Well, that befuddles me."

To Flynn it did not seem like that much of a job for a man who had been trusted by his government at a major money conference at The Hague eighteen years before, at the age of thirty-three.

Then Flynn remembered that he himself was now mainly employed as a Boston policeman, and he had been at that same conference at the age of twenty-two.

Flynn said, "Isn't current social mobility a wonder to behold?"

He took three bills from his pocket—a twenty-, a fifty-, and a hundred-dollar bill—and handed them to Paul Sankey.

"I would like to have the highest authority in the land assure me of the authenticity of these little darlings. There's a wee suspicion abroad they're not the legitimate children of Mama Treasury and Papa Justice."

Holding the bills in his hand, Sankey looked disappointed. "You mean, are they counterfeit?"

"That's the question."

Sankey sniffed them, and looked at them again, closely. "They look all right to me, but I'll have them tested." Finally, he smiled. "I just remembered you and I having a dinner together at The Hague. Whatever it was we ordered, all we got was heaps of sauerkraut." He put the bills in his shirt pocket. "What's this about, Flynn?"

"What's what about?"

"You didn't need to come directly to Special Section to have a few bills tested for authenticity."

"Ach, well," Flynn said. "That. I had to come to Washington anyway. There are some people I need to see at the Pentagon this afternoon."

"No," Sankey said. "I learned my lesson with you eighteen years ago. You're not worrying about one hundred and seventy dollars in counterfeit money."

"Aren't I?"

"No."

"Oh." Flynn rose. Neither of them had touched his coffee or roll. "It's a mysterious matter."

Sankey said, "I expect so."

"Great sums of money have been turning up in odd places."

" 'Great sums'?"

"Over four hundred million dollars."

Sankey stood up. He headed tiredly toward the door. "I'll have these bills checked out for you, Flynn. Where can I reach you?"

"Hotel Dorland. I hope to be there only until tomorrow morning."

"All right."

"Please leave the message for me at the desk. There seems to be some confusion as to which room I'm in."

"Oh? How can there be?"

"Exactly."

Sankey opened the door for Flynn. "One day I wouldn't mind understanding you, Flynn. Or having you understand me."

"Sure," Flynn said. "Frequently I feel the same way myself."

20

"**I** have been over this ground a dozen times, Mister Flynn."

There was no fat on the body of Major William Calder.

Flynn had found the major finishing a heavy workout in a gymnasium of the Pentagon, and accepted his invitation to join him in the sauna.

They were alone.

Flynn smiled. "Surely a military man like yourself is used to doing things in triplicate."

Calder's look could be read as that of the usual military sentry: no one is permitted to get under the skin of the military, except military personnel.

"I've been ordered to answer your questions, Mister Flynn. I'll answer them. I'm just saying I'm sick and angry over this whole ball of wax."

"Why is that?"

The major looked as if he had just been ordered to eat a bowl of live garden snakes for national security reasons.

"We were a good outfit. A good team. Blown all to hell and back."

"You mean United States Air Force Intelligence Section 11B."

Flynn's specific identification of the department caused the major to wince before he admitted, "Yeah."

Flynn had observed that all American military departments—especially the Intelligence sections—thought it was they and only they who had the world on a string. None did.

"We were doing good work," added the major.

"What specifically were you doing at that point in time?"

The major's look was wary.

"You know you're authorized to tell me."

In fact, earlier in the afternoon Flynn had been thoroughly filled in by the Pentagon team investigating this matter.

"Our responsibility was constant surveillance, assimilation, and interpretation of all air units both sides of the Sino-Soviet border."

"An important job," said Flynn. "But not one you'd expect to come up in conversation too often, I think. In this job, Major, was anything peculiarly important going on at the time that—?"

"Of course."

"I mean, anything unusual? Was anything coming to a head, do you think?"

"I don't think I understand you."

"Was anything unusual happening on the Sino-Soviet border, as you perceived things?"

"Troops both sides of the Sino-Soviet border are in constant movement. It's a big sparring match—the biggest in the world. One side moves a battalion twelve hundred kilometers north; the other side moves two battalions one thousand kilometers south; the first side moves a full wing two thousand kilometers south."

"And what does that all mean?"

"It's a war of nerves. A training ground for both troops and strategists."

"How do you understand it?"

"Easily. The Russians are playing chess and the Chinese are playing Mah-Jongg."

"Expensive games."

"It's been going on for years."

"And you say nothing unusual was happening?"

"Why do you ask, Mister Flynn?"

"Obviously, Major, if a department like yours was blinded, the sensible question is: what was it someone didn't want you to see?"

"Oh." The major compared his feet on the tile floor. "No. There was nothing unusual going on. As far as I know. In fact," he looked rather brightly at Flynn, "both sides were repeating a pattern of maneuvers they had gone through, exactly, eighteen months before. We wondered if they knew it."

Flynn grinned. "Maybe you should have phoned them up and told them. Save them the bother."

"Yeah."

Flynn toweled the sweat off his back. "So one fine day, a Saturday morning, you leave your house, whistling a merry tune, golf bag in tow, and there on the front seat of your car is a big manila envelope with one hundred thousand of the good ones in it."

"Right."

"You had not locked your car overnight?"

"No. Betty and I had been out late at a party the night before. I guess I forgot."

"Were there other cars parked in the immediate vicinity? I mean, was the car in a parking lot?"

"No. It was in the carport of our house. In Alexandria."

"What was the first thing you did?"

"I went back in the house and called Major Williger."

"Who's Major Williger?"

"The guy I was going to play golf with. I told him I had to cancel. I gave him some bull. I think I told him Betty was sick, and I had to stay home and take care of the kids."

"Not true?"

"Not true."

"Did the major believe you?"

"I suppose so."

"Major, you mean you didn't go racing back into the house, dropping golf clubs as you ran, shouting at your wife you'd just found a young fortune in your carport?"

"No. I never mentioned it to my wife."

"Good heavens, why not, man?"

"I guess I immediately assumed it had something to do with my capacity as an Intelligence officer."

"That was your immediate reaction?"

"I never thought otherwise. We're trained, Mister Flynn, to consider anything unusual as potentially threatening to our Intelligence function. Anything. And, you agree, this was unusual."

"Indeed it was. What did you do then?"

"I went into the den and closed the door and tried to get General Seiler on the phone."

"Your commanding officer?"

"Yes."

"You were going to report the incident?"

"Yes. His wife answered the phone. She sounded funny. She said the general was unavailable and would remain unavailable. So I called Colonel Perham. His wife said he'd gone hunting for the weekend. On Monday morning I discovered they had both spent the weekend filing for early retirement."

"Apparently they hadn't been as well trained as you," Flynn said, "to consider anything unusual as potentially threatening to their Intelligence capacity."

"Or they didn't care."

"What did you do then?"

"I called Colonel Seely. His wife said Bob was out buying a boat. Bob had never mentioned an interest in sailing to me. He's a skeet-shooting nut."

"You didn't tell your wife about it all weekend?"

"I never told her. I still haven't told her."

"What reason did you give her for canceling your golf date?"

"I said I had a hangover. From the party the night before. Couldn't stand the sun."

"I see. And then, Monday morning . . . ?"

"General Seiler and Colonel Perham were running around with retirement papers in their hands. Colonel Seely was unresponsive."

"You mean, you mentioned the matter to him?"

"Yes."

"What did he say?"

"He said, 'Well, Bill, it's a short life and we shouldn't miss out on it through an unwarranted sense of self-importance.' "

"I see. He had been a particular friend of yours?"

"We had worked pretty closely together."

"Then what did you do?"

"I blew the whistle. I called Section 1. Air Force Intelligence Command."

Gently, Flynn asked, "And what has happened since then?"

Sadly, slowly, Major William Calder said, "We all got reassigned. One way or the other."

Earlier that afternoon, Flynn had been briefed by the investigating team on what had happened to the individuals of U.S.A.F.I.S. 11B.

GENERAL JOHN SEILER. Retired. Pension withheld until completion of investigation. The general and his wife of twenty-six years separated. She remained in Washington. He was currently living in Ponce, Puerto Rico.

COLONEL JOHN PERHAM. Retired. Pension withheld until completion of investigation. The colonel had gained forty-five pounds in weight.

COLONEL ROBERT SEELY. Currently in Walter Reed Hospital Psychiatric Diagnostic Center, having suffered a nervous breakdown.

MAJOR SAMUEL ROSENSTONE. Transferred to United States Armed Forces Staff College in Norfolk, Virginia, as an instructor in Air Base Perimeter Security.

On and on, through the sixty-seven members of that department. The chief secretary, Adele Hughes, had come to suffer chronic high blood pressure. Hulett Weed, the technician clerk who eloped on that weekend, left his honeymoon bed the next Friday morning before dawn, without his bride, and was currently on the *Whereabouts Unknown* list.

Major Calder said, "I've been reassigned to Supply." He shook his head. "Do anything unusual in the military, anything unusual happens to you, your career gets sidetracked *permanently*."

"Lieutenant DuPont also was quick to report finding a bundle of money in his mailbox. What happened to him?"

"He's left the service," Calder said. "He saw what was happening to him. He was reassigned to work with an Air Force wrestling team as an assistant coach."

"Sometimes being honest is a mistake?"

"Oh, it's no mistake," answered Calder. "But sometimes it just hurts like hell."

"It does that," said Flynn. "It does that. My God, this place is as hot as Texas without the wind."

Calder smiled. "Shall I open a window?"

"I think I've had enough sauna," said Flynn, gathering up his towels. "I'd hate to leave too much of myself here at the Pentagon. Just one more question, Major. You're trained in Intelligence work. Why did this happen? Why was everyone in your department given a large amount of money anonymously?"

The major shrugged. "Someone wanted to blow up that department."

"But why?"

The major just shrugged.

"You said there was nothing, as far as you know, going on in the world at that moment for anyone to want to render that department ineffective."

"That's what I said, Mister Flynn." The major

shook sweat out of his curly hair. "Maybe someone just wanted to prove you could buy off a Pentagon Intelligence section with a corned beef sandwich and a glass of beer."

Standing, Flynn said, "Now, who would want to do that, I wonder?"

Under heavy, wet eyebrows Major Calder looked up at him. "Three possibilities: the Russians; the Chinese; or . . . some other American Intelligence section."

"I see," said Flynn. "I see. You mean, someone might spend as much as three and a half million dollars on internecine Pentagon squabbling?"

Major Calder said: "More has been spent on less, Mister Flynn. More has been spent on less."

Just after seven o'clock that night, Flynn approached the reception desk at the Hotel Dorland.

"Ah, Mister Flynn!" the desk clerk said. "Checking in again?"

"I've never checked out, you blithering—"

"That's never made a difference before," the desk clerk said.

"Delighted I am to find you in good humor," Flynn said.

"Ah, well, we all have our little aberrations, haven't we?"

"I'm here to ask if there are any messages for me."

"There is." The desk clerk reached into a room box behind him. "Just one."

Flynn took the folded piece of paper. Then he said to the desk clerk, with full seriousness, "I wonder if you'd have a Saint Bernard sent to my room?"

The desk clerk blinked. "A Saint Bernard?"

"That's what I said."

"You mean, a large dog?"

"Yes," said Flynn. "A Saint Bernard is a large dog."

The desk clerk's right hand shook. "Of course, Mister Flynn. I'll have one sent right up."

"Thank you."

Crossing the lobby to the elevator, Flynn read the message:

> *Please call me at my home as soon as you get in.* 555-8708. *I want private discussion with you.*
>
> —*Paul Sankey.*

21

"Think me a dull fellow if you want," Paul Sankey said, "but I'm still chewing over that statement you snuck into the ambassador's speech eighteen years ago: 'The European Common Market will never attain an economic force equal to that of the United States of America. It is in full cognizance of this that the United States of America assures European Common Market nations of the full support of the United States of America.'"

"You've got it down pat."

"Flynn, do you realize what has happened since?"

Flynn only realized he was about to be lectured.

He had arrived at Paul Sankey's house by taxi at nine-thirty at night. They had agreed to meet at nine o'clock, but it had taken the taxi driver a long time to find the address.

Paul Sankey lived in the middle of an obscure alley in the Georgetown section of Washington. It was the smallest house Flynn had ever seen in any city. It was too small even to have served as a coach house or garage.

When Sankey opened the door to him, Flynn found himself in what appeared to be the only room on that floor. It was not a living room, in the usual sense. There was one comfortable chair and footstool. Stacks of books were everywhere on the floor. The walls were lined with drafting tables. On each there was what appeared to be a graph-in-progress. On the walls above hung huge graphs, each with its own color scheme, red, blue, green, brown. Flynn guessed all the graphs had to do with economic analysis. Fluorescent lights hung from the ceiling. In the fireplace, stacked one on the other, were two small filing cases.

Flynn had been shown to the one comfortable chair. He was not offered food or drink.

Sankey, in shirt-sleeves and tie, remained standing. He immediately began speaking in the most earnest terms.

"That statement," Sankey said, "uttered by that person, the ambassador, at that time, eighteen years ago, at that place, The Hague, destroyed the world as you and I knew it."

Flynn suspected it had destroyed the world as Paul Sankey knew it—Paul Sankey's world.

"You don't know much about economics, do you, Flynn. Despite your unholy interference in it."

"It hasn't been proved I interfered," Flynn said mildly.

"Oh, you did, all right. You or whoever you were working for. You changed the world."

Flynn shrugged blamelessly. Sankey was a bitter man. Flynn might as well give him his moment to yowl.

"All right." Stepping around the small room, Sankey punctuated his remarks with jabs of his index finger at various charts on the walls.

"Post–World War II economic recovery plans were designed to result in a group of more or less equal economic entities—the United States, the European Common Market, a Latin American Common Market, the British Commonwealth Nations. Now, many things

went wrong with this plan, but one thing in particular
—traceable to that statement you fed into the ambassador's speech eighteen years ago at The Hague.

"According to that statement, no matter how many
'equals' were set up, no matter how powerful they
were individually or together, the United States would
dominate the world's economy. Do you see how unfair
this was?"

Flynn shrugged. "It would seem to have been a
candid statement," Flynn said, "for the time."

"All right." Sankey was running his index finger
over a specific graph on the wall that made no sense
whatsoever to Flynn. "To be very simple. First, under
this new economic scheme, the world goes off the gold
standard. Instead, what will be used is a currency established and backed by the International Monetary
Fund, called S.D.R.'s or Special Drawing Rights. All
this is news to you?"

"Not precisely," said Flynn.

"Only that's not what happened. Because the
United States dominated the world's economy, the rest
of the world went off the gold standard and onto the
dollar standard."

Sankey moved on to another chart.

"Only that's not what happened, either. The dollar
was backed by American resources—which were not
as infinite as American arrogance. The United States
began running out of resources, particularly that resource which is 'liquid gold' to every industrial nation
on earth—oil."

Sankey flicked his fingernails against his chart.
"Therefore, the world went from the gold standard to
a dollar standard to an oil standard—an oil-paid-for-
in-dollars standard.

"Trouble is, Flynn, oil is an exhaustible commodity.

"Can you imagine a world in which the economy's
basic commodity—that which is the standard for all

133

currencies—is poured into people's automobiles and furnaces and burned?"

Sankey's eyes had become slightly red-rimmed.

Flynn said, "All this is very edifyin', I'm sure." He began to pack his pipe.

"Flynn, did you realize that the oil-producing nations—at least, the cartel, OPEC—accepted payment for oil only in dollars?"

Flynn put his tobacco pouch back in his pocket. "I guess I did."

"By the time the International Monetary Fund's Managing Director, H. Johannes Witteveen, began insisting the world go back to the original plan and use S.D.R.'s instead of dollars, there was a half-trillion out there floating around the world. A half-trillion dollars, Flynn. Any idea what that means?"

"None whatsoever."

"Of course you don't."

"I still twitch at the sight of a twenty-dollar bill, folded."

"Now let me ask you this: how could the United States, or any nation, foist a half-trillion dollars in paper currency on the world?"

Flynn answered nothing. His pipe was drawing nicely.

Sankey stepped to another chart. "First, to keep a strong economic image, the United States allowed its principal corporations to grow to mammoth size. It allowed them to become world monopolies, figuratively if not literally.

"Look what happened without competition: from 1947 to 1964 the production worker's average gain in productivity was 4.12 percent. From 1964 to 1975, the rate dropped to 1.65 percent. Are you familiar with the work of Byung Yoo Hung?"

"Can't say that I am," said Flynn.

"As worker productivity lowered"—Sankey ran his finger along a graph curve—"below growth and efficiency levels, American business had no choice but to switch from a cost-offsetting basis to a cost-pass-along strategy, to maintain profits."

"Ye Gods." Flynn stifled a yawn.

"Expense to the consumer began accelerating. Management cut back on their capital spending. Technological development slowed down."

"Some fellow, that Byung Yoo Hung."

"I'm making all this very simple for you."

"I can tell."

"If you'd just study these charts."

"I'm studying," said Flynn from his chair. "I'm studying."

"Second, to maintain this strong image abroad, essentially United States capital was shifted from the civilian economy to military hardware." Sankey came closer to Flynn and hissed, "There was oil off Vietnam, Flynn."

"I'd heard."

Sankey nodded to him as if he had made a most telling point, and then went back to his wall charts.

"Have you heard of the Laffer Curve?" Sankey asked.

"Who hasn't?"

Sankey pointed to a chart which looked like the business end of a bullet, upended.

"As inflation increased, everyone ascended into higher tax brackets. Everyone's taxes increased. Even though everyone's income increased, everyone's purchasing power decreased."

"Don't I know it, though?" said Flynn, thinking of his five children.

"Through inflation and taxes, the government was taking more out of the economy than the amount that would permit the economy to continue running profitably. Flynn, it's rather like a shopkeeper who keeps taking so much money out of his cash register to live on and duck next door for a beer, that when the time comes he doesn't have the money to restock his shelves."

"Thank you very much for this lesson in economics," Flynn said. "Is it over?"

Sankey said, "I guess it is."

Flynn said, "Whew."

"There are other results," Sankey said. "The expense of government itself. There are too many governments—federal, state, county, city, borough or town—duplicating each other. One out of seven people in the United States now derives his income from the government. Regulations. The United States Congress passes fifty thousand pages of new laws a year."

"You make it all sound like a hopeless mess," said Flynn. "I don't get the point. I don't understand why you called me over here when I could happily be in bed with a book to tell me the world's economy isn't all it should be."

"Let me put it this way, Flynn: eighteen years ago I was one of a large group who did not expect the United States to try to dominate the world's economy. Chickens always come home to roost."

"And you think I—a mere slip of a boy, hardly present at all—slipped something into your ambassador's speech eighteen years ago that's been ticking away like a time bomb ever since and now is causing a grand, worldwide economic upheaval, if not disaster."

Sankey said, "Yes."

"Well, you're fighting old battles, lad."

"The point I'm trying to make tonight is that I'm not fighting old battles. A statement eighteen years ago, a direction taken, is causing pain and suffering tonight."

Flynn stood up. "What I know about economics," he said, "is that things go up and things go down: they never stay the same." Flynn waved his hand at the walls. "If any of you chaps who draws graphs ever knew what you were talking about life would be a bowl of vanilla ice cream. Economists," Flynn said, "are people who take care of their own personal economies by forever mouthing doom and gloom."

"I'm just a government worker, Flynn."

"I see that. One who has to grab people in from off the street to test out petty theories. You just gave me a funeral oration while the patient's simply breathing a little hard."

"Sorry you didn't understand it."

"Why don't you just give me the answer to the question I asked, man, instead of all this gobbledygook about the world's economy?"

"What question did you ask?"

"Are those bills I gave you real or fake?"

"Oh, that."

"That!" expostulated Flynn. "That and nothing more."

Sankey took the three bills from his shirt pocket and handed them to Flynn.

Sankey said, "The one-hundred-dollar bill is real; the fifty-dollar bill is real; the twenty-dollar bill is fake."

"Flies to a dead man's eyes!" said Flynn. "Even to that I can't get an answer that says yes or no, but only an answer somewhere in between! The Lord save us all from those who make the noises of intellectuals!"

He looked at the bills in his hand.

Sankey said, "The most common counterfeit bill in the United States is the twenty-dollar bill."

"What are you saying, man?"

"I'm saying that in any pack of twenty-dollar bills, chances are higher that one of them is counterfeit than there would be in any other denomination."

"Oh. I see. These other two bills are not fake, as far as your best experts can discover, and it means nothin' at all that the twenty-dollar bill is fake?"

"That's right."

"Tell me, Mister Sankey: is it possible perfect counterfeits could be made? Counterfeits so perfect even your best experts couldn't tell they're fake?"

"Of course."

"Yes?"

"Absolutely. Anything made by human hands and machinery can be duplicated perfectly by other human hands and machinery."

"You don't publicize that fact too much, do you?" Sankey smiled. "No."

"Do you think people have counterfeited American money and never gotten caught?"

"I know they have."

"How do you know it?"

"Because there's always slightly more currency in the market than the Federal Reserve Bank generates."

"There is?"

"Always."

"Much?"

"No. Producing a lot of counterfeit money is the sure way to get caught. A lot of money coming from nowhere would be noticed. It would involve too many people."

"It would be the sure way to be caught," said Flynn, "except maybe this once."

"What do you mean?"

"Except maybe this last time."

"If it's any consolation, I don't understand you either, Flynn."

"Ach, sure, I don't understand myself." He put the bills into his pocket. "I have a problem. I'm not solving it. Sure, and doesn't it make me grumpy, though?" He shook hands with Paul Sankey. "I thank you for a charmin' evenin'. I'm sure I learned something, but I'm not sure what."

This time, Sankey shook hands with him.

"Odd wee house, this," said Flynn.

"It's everything I need."

"Is it?" Flynn peered around him. "Is it all of that?"

"There's a kitchen in the basement, this room on the first floor, and a bedroom and a bath upstairs.

"Built for a herd of leprechauns, was it?"

"I don't know what it was built for," Sankey said. "But you wouldn't believe the price I could get for it —on today's market."

"I daresay," said Flynn. "Sure, it would make a nice embassy for the Republic of Ifad."

Sankey smiled. "There is a Republic of Ifad?"

"Don't worry," said Flynn. "They have no economy at all. But why did I have the impression you have a wife and children? Daughters, wasn't it? I remember your mentioning them that time over cabbage at The Hague. You showed me pictures, I think. . . ."

Sankey's expression was grim. "I had a wife and daughters."

Flynn said, "Oh."

"They were killed. Automobile accident. Outside National Airport. Six years ago."

Flynn said, "I'm sorry."

"They were hit by a three-axle army truck, driven by drunken soldiers."

Flynn said nothing.

"And do you know what the army truck was doing there, Flynn? It was delivering twelve dozen fresh flowers for a cocktail party at the Pentagon. A three-axle truck speeding one hundred and forty-four flowers to the Pentagon killed my wife and daughters."

Flynn said, "I'm sorry for you, man."

Sankey opened the front door.

"Good night," Flynn said. "Thanks for the instruction. Next time the economy comes up at my dinner table I'll appear a wee bit smarter in front of my children, I will."

After Sankey closed the door, the alley was without any light.

After a few cautious steps, Flynn tripped over a packing case and fell against a rubbish barrel.

"Damn," he said. "And it wasn't even myself who slipped those words into the ambassador's speech. And I wonder who did, seeing they were so damned important?"

22

"You can't get there from here."

The eyes of the ancient man filling the gas tank of Flynn's rented jeep darted from the pump's gauge to Flynn and back again, to see if his witticism was enjoyed or even recognized.

"I can't get to Cleary's Mountain, or I mayn't?"

"You may, but you can't," the old man said. "You won't."

"Why is that?"

"Are they expecting you?"

"No."

The man hung up the gasoline nozzle.

"I didn't think so. Anybody expected at Cleary's Mountain comes in by plane or helicopter. The only vehicles that use that road are George Udine's own. Besides the trucks haulin' lumber down, only other thing you see on that road is one of the Cleary Mountain Land Rovers. Servants out for a toot. Every year or so."

Flynn handed the old man his credit card. "You're saying I can't get in."

"Maybe if you had the wings of an angel." The

old man looked at Flynn's shoulders. "Which I don't think you do. Electrified chain-link fence, deep in the ground, barbs on top, all around the mountain. Uniformed guards with shotguns and attack dogs patrolling inside the fence. Ol' George likes his privacy."

"You've never seen him?"

The old man shook his head as he handed Flynn the credit slip to sign. "Ol' George is sort of quiet, as neighbors go."

"Still and all." Flynn handed the signed slip back to him. "Where's the road up to the place?"

"Go down here two miles and take the loggin' road to your left. It'll take you about a half-hour just to get to the fence."

The old man started back to his chair in the shade of the gas shack. "I'll see you comin' back in about an hour, I guess. I'll wave at you as you go by."

Flynn slowed as he approached the fence around Cleary's Mountain.

The gate was wide open.

He stopped in it and looked around.

No uniformed guards. No trained attack dogs.

He blew his horn.

No one.

"My, my." Flynn put the jeep into low gear and continued along the logging road up Cleary's Mountain.

There was a haze of smoke halfway up the mountain.

The house on a high shoulder of Cleary's Mountain was a sprawling, mammoth log and fieldstone structure.

In the parking lot across from the main door were two yellow Land Rovers.

Flynn parked his jeep next to them.

The smell of smoke was not as strong here as it had been while he was coming up the mountain.

The view of Oregon's mountains was stunning. He

was just below the tree line. Flynn figured he could see two hundred kilometers to the east, north, and south. Trees and mountain tops. Not a roof or a road in sight. To the north a few kilometers were wide, slow-moving clouds of smoke.

A woman with the face of an axe answered the door after Flynn had rung several times.

"Yes?"

Flynn said, "I'm here to see George Udine."

She looked around the parking lot behind him. "Did they let you through the main gate?"

Flynn gave his beguiling smile. "They didn't keep me out."

"I was wondering. . . . Usually they send someone up, to escort you. . . ."

Flynn too looked around the empty parking lot.

"Well," she said. "There's a fire somewhere on the place. They probably couldn't spare a man to send with you."

Flynn maintained the wisdom of silence.

"Mr. Udine isn't here."

"No?"

"He's down at the Shack. Down at the lake. There's no phone down there." The axe almost cracked a smile. "It's his getaway place."

"I'm sure he needs one," said Flynn.

She leaned out of the doorway and pointed around the building. "If you just follow that road down, it will lead you to the Shack. You'll see his Land Rover. It has a number one on it. Of course he may be out on the lake. . . ."

"I'll find it," Flynn said. "Thank you, ma'am."

Going down the road, Flynn went through three pockets of smoke so thick he had to slow the jeep to a crawl. His eyes watered and even with a handkerchief over his nose and mouth, he found himself coughing.

There was no smoke in the immediate environs of the Shack.

The Shack: Flynn guessed it was a twelve- to fifteen-room house. Rustic. With neatly clipped lawns and tended flower gardens. On the edge of a high, blue lake. Surrounded by forests and mountain peaks.

In its graveled parking lot was a yellow Land Rover. On its hood was a red figure one in a red circle.

"So," said Flynn. "This is where George Udine is when he's at home."

The door was open so Flynn went in, saying, "Hello? Hello?"

He followed the corridor into a bright, well-furnished living room.

A man in his early sixties, dressed in a plaid lumberjack's shirt, brown slacks, and sport shoes, was in the room, leaning over a wide windowsill, tying flies.

Flynn stood in the doorway.

"George Udine?"

The man didn't look up.

"Yes?"

"Also George Lewis?"

He still didn't look up, but his response was slower.

"Yes?"

"From Ada, Texas?"

Finally the man looked at Flynn.

"What do you want?"

Instead of the imposing figure Flynn had expected, George Udine had the face and body of an attractive young boy who had faded, slowly, ever so slowly, into being sixty years old. His hair was thin but still sandy. Liver spots gave the impression of freckles. His eyes were a chocolate brown. He was a little less than average height, and still slim.

Flynn ambled into the room and sat down in an armchair.

"I saw your mother a few days ago."

"That old whore still alive?"

George Udine returned his attention to tying flies.

Flynn said, "They call her the 'pig woman.' "

"That's about right," Udine said. "She's a pig. And I guess she's a woman."

Flynn said, "She lives in a tar-paper shack in a gully off the main road out of Ada, Texas. She dresses in a ball gown and glass earrings and necklaces and bracelets and tends her pigs and her chickens and her cats."

George Udine chuckled. "I hardly remember her. She must be about eighty now. Surprised to hear she's still alive."

"There's a rumor around," Flynn said, "that she had a son, named George, who ran off and became a very rich man."

"That's right, I guess. Although how anybody down there would know about it, I don't know."

"They don't believe it," Flynn said.

"Good," George Udine said. "Good."

Flynn took out his pipe and tobacco pouch and then put them away again. He had had enough smoke in his lungs.

"I haven't seen her in over fifty years," George Udine said. "Over half a century. I haven't thought of her twice in half that time."

Through the windows of the living room Flynn saw a terrace overlooking the dock and the lake. There was a cabin cruiser at the dock, and a two-meter rowboat.

"You have a yacht?" Flynn asked. "I mean, an oceangoing yacht?"

"Yeah, I have one somewhere. I think it's in the Bahamas right now. I think I lent it to somebody. The president of something. Some country."

"Two years ago you were cruising in your yacht and you stopped for the night in East Frampton, Massachusetts."

"Did I?"

"And you didn't go ashore?"

"Probably not. Lobster restaurants. Fat people with too much sunburn. Taxis in unlikely colors. Why should anyone go ashore?"

"Did anything unusual happen to you that night?"

"I don't even remember being . . . wherever you said I was."

"East Frampton, Massachusetts."

"Wherever."

"Have you been there before or since?"

"I don't know. Two summers ago I cruised New England's waters. I had before. I haven't since."

"East Frampton, Massachusetts, means nothing to you?"

"I'm not aware of ever having heard of the place."

"And you haven't seen your mother in over fifty years?"

"In the wisdom of my youth, I left her to the pigs."

"Have you never been back to Ada, Texas?"

"Never."

"Do you hate your mother? Do you hate Ada, Texas?"

"I have nothing but indifference for both. Complete indifference. Does that disappoint you?"

Flynn smelled smoke.

" 'Crazy old Mrs. Lewis,' as she's called, and Ada, Texas, are where you came from."

George Udine shrugged. "What's your pinch?"

" 'Pinch'?"

"How are you going to hit me up? Blackmail me with photos of my mother in a ball gown feeding pigs? Hell with it. I was born without concern for what people think of me. Or are you just here out of the goodness of your heart to see if I might spring some cash her way, to provide her with decent living and care? I won't. I only spent nine or so years with the bitch, but she did not provide me with decent living and care. I remember that."

"That doesn't sound like 'complete indifference' to me," Flynn said. "That sounds like bitterness."

" 'Bitterness'? Bullshit. I left her to the pigs more than fifty years ago, and I've never looked back. I'll never do anything for her. There are a lot of people

I don't care about I'll never do anything for. That about includes everybody. Including you. Whatever you came here for, fella, you're not going to get it."

Through the windows there was no sign of the smoke.

"A while ago," Flynn said, "someone gave your mother one hundred thousand dollars in cash."

Udine snorted. "Great. What did she do, feed it to the pigs?"

"Not yet. She was quick to hand it over to a stranger, though."

"Sure she was."

"Odd thing is, someone gave everyone in Ada, Texas, one hundred thousand dollars in cash."

"Everyone?"

"Every man, woman, and child."

"I didn't."

"Could you have? Could you afford to do a thing like that?"

"I suppose so."

"Everyone in East Frampton, Massachusetts, got one hundred thousand dollars in cash."

Udine said, "Pretty upsetting to their economy, I should think."

"Why would anyone do a thing like that, Mister Udine?"

"I've lived my life upon one principle, and it's never been proven wrong: everyone is crazy."

"You've never been proven wrong?"

"Not once."

"What would be even a crazy reason for doing it, Mister Udine?"

George Udine thought about it, while continuing to tie flies.

"I don't know."

Flynn stood up and headed for the door.

George Udine said, "Is that all you wanted? To see if I was the one who gave one hundred thousand bucks each to the people in Ada and . . . wherever else?"

"Yes. That's all."

"I can assure you," George Udine said, with a charming smile on his handsome face, "I have never voluntarily done charity in my life. I never will."

Flynn said, "Thanks."

Then he stood a moment longer, looking at George Udine in profile against the window.

"One other question, Mister Udine."

Udine did not answer.

"I was in Washington last night. A man, a government bureaucrat who seemed to know his potatoes, gave me quite a lecture on the world's economy."

"He said it was falling apart, didn't he?"

"He did."

"And he was very convincing."

"He was."

"They always are."

"Who are?"

"Doomsayers. I'll guarantee you that at any time in history you can find people with scriptures, with maps, with charts, with astrological forecasts, all of which absolutely prove—at least to them and whoever else they can get to take them seriously—that the world is falling apart."

"And it never is?"

"It never has yet."

"Mister Udine: is the world's economy in good shape?"

Udine grinned at him. "Mine is."

At the door, Flynn turned again to Udine. "Don't you smell smoke?"

Udine sniffed. "There's probably a fire somewhere on the place."

23

Turning the key in the ignition of his jeep, Flynn marveled that never once had George Udine expressed the slightest curiosity about him. Udine had not asked Flynn his name, where he was from, or whom he represented. He had not even asked how Flynn had gotten through Cleary Mountain's electrified fence, patrolling guards, and attack dogs.

"That," said Flynn, "is an indifferent man."

He was only five hundred meters down the road from the Shack when something leaped across the road in front of him, high up, from tree to tree, something almost human in its leap, like a ballet dancer, but more than human in its speed.

He braked.

Both sides of the road were blazing fire.

By the time he turned around on the narrow dirt road, the fire, red, vicious, crackling, had caught up to the rear of the jeep. There was a rush of wind. Accelerating hard did not drown out the noise of the wind rushing and the trees snapping, falling through each other, crashing to the ground.

Flynn left the jeep in front of the house, pounded

up the steps, along the corridor, and into the living room.

"Let's go," he said.

George Udine looked up.

"Quick! Fire! The wind is this way."

George Udine laughed, softly.

Flynn yelled, "Will you move, man?"

Udine rose slowly from the window seat. "Where are we going?"

"To the middle of the lake."

All the way down the dock, Flynn had to hustle Udine along. He wasn't sure whether Udine didn't believe him, didn't like taking orders, or simply was indifferent to whatever would happen.

Once on the dock, they saw the smoke climbing, rising high above the house.

Udine began to get into the cabin cruiser, while Flynn was untying the rowboat.

"Not that," Flynn shouted. "It has gas in it."

Udine, moving a little more quickly, joined Flynn in the rowboat.

Flynn pulled hard for the middle of the lake.

The north shore of the lake was a wall of fire.

There was enough wind from the fire to stir up the surface of the water.

Ashes were falling on them.

Sitting on the stern thwart, George Udine watched the fire with an odd, appreciative smile on his face: a boy granted a special fireworks display for his birthday.

Flynn got to the middle of the lake and rested on his oars.

There was too much noise from the fire for them to speak.

Under the smoke, the light had turned to an eerie, deep dusk.

Flynn coughed.

He was surprised to see how thick with ashes the bottom of the boat and the surface of the water were.

He spun the boat around so he could see the fire and the house better, making George Udine pivot on his seat to watch.

After a while, from the other side of the house there was a boom and then another boom. Flynn guessed the jeep and Land Rover had blown up.

He kept his eye on the house, the Shack.

The cabin cruiser at the dock exploded first.

Then there were flames in the windows of the Shack, oddly enough the second story first; then the walls blew out, collapsing the roof.

After a minute, Flynn shouted, "I guess you lost your house."

Udine said, "I have seven others. No, eight. No . . . seven."

Shouting had caused Flynn to cough smoke out of his throat and lungs.

The two men were to sit in the rowboat a long time, watching the fire. At times the smoke was so thick they had to duck their heads toward the bottom of the boat to find air to breathe.

Night fell.

Tall-stemmed, red-blossomed flowers of fire ran through the forests on all sides of them.

I'll never be over it, will I? Flynn's voice began inside his head. *Me, coming home to the little apartment in Munich—the Irish Consulate, it was, a modest enough place, a living room, two bedrooms, a bath, a kitchen—me, in my short pants and neckerchief of Hitler Youth, after standing an air raid watch—finding the both of them, my mother and my father, on the floor of the kitchen, each shot between the eyes. . .*

Were they shot as an arbitrary thing, a gratuitous act in those last, frantic, insane days of the war when there was so much suffering and death around there was as little resistance to shooting another person as there ever is to shaking a hand and saying something pleasant?

Or were they shot for good reason, because it had

been discovered that the Irish Consul and his wife had been smuggling American and British fliers out of the country, home to fight again, on their own good time? That the wee son of the Irish Consul and his wife, me in the neckerchief and short pants, had been keeping up correspondence in my schoolboy scrawl with my own chums in Ireland, Master Timothy O'Brien and Master William Cavanaugh, who existed only as names on letter boxes at British Intelligence, London?

Were they shot for good reason, or just shot?

Sometimes I've thought I'd give the rest of my life to know the answer to that question.

Then the weeks and months, living in the streets.

It was never the bombs that bothered. They just came. It was the fires, the constant fires, acrid smoke always in the back of the nose, the top of the throat, the special smell of human bodies burning; sleeping against the stone wall of a building and having the heat of it burn you awake, you knowing there was fire the other side of that wall whether you could see it or hear it or smell it or not; once, being surrounded by fire—like this—helping people to pry up a sewer lid from the road, and then lowering ourselves, one by one, into the sewage of the City of Munich. The filthy stuff was up to my chin.

It's the fires I'll never be over. . . .

It was after midnight.

Francis Xavier Flynn and George Udine sat in the small rowboat, still roughly in the middle of the lake, having said very little to each other. On the surface of the lake the smoke had cleared only slightly. No stars or moon were visible through the mantle of smoke that hung over them. On the shore, all sides of them, against the mountain walls, thousands of small fires were still blazing along their own courses. Occasionally one would flare for a brilliant moment. They were their own world in their own galaxy.

Soot was in Flynn's hair, his eyes, his nose, his mouth.

Several times they had stirred the water with their hands and scooped some into their mouths.

Flynn said, "Rub-a-dub-dub."

After a moment, Udine said, "I've been thinking about your friend in Washington. The prophet of gloom and doom. The soothsayer."

"The economist."

"Inflation is an event," said George Udine, "just like a war or a depression, usually leading to either or both."

Flynn had trouble seeing Udine through the gloom. He said, "I thought inflation could lead only to deflation."

Udine said, "Money is only as good as people's belief in it."

"May I quote that?"

"Money is only an idea. There are lots of ideas: religious ideas, political ideas. People build their ideas slowly, but confront them with one catastrophe and they discard their ideas in the blink of a eye. I don't trust ideas."

"You don't believe in money?"

"No. Of course not. It's excrement."

Flynn said, "You've collected a considerable amount of excrement."

"I make money," George Udine said, "because other people believe in it. I collect garbage because pigs want to eat it. Money is a convenient medium of exchange."

Shortly after three o'clock in the morning, Flynn heard the cawing of a crow.

Flynn seldom believed what he heard, but he always believed his ears.

"Tell me," Flynn said. "How did George Lewis, son of Ada's pig woman, become George Udine of the

Udine Corporation, Cleary's Mountain, or what's left of it, and seven or eight other places around the world?"

For many minutes there was no answer.

Flynn would not ask him again.

Long after Flynn had decided there would be no answer, George Udine began talking.

"I said money is a convenient medium of exchange."

"I got that part," Flynn answered.

"I left Ada, Texas."

"Nearly everyone has."

"I was nine and a half, ten years old. Like everything else about me," said the apparently disembodied voice, "I am free to decide the precise moment of my birth. The event not only didn't shake the world, it didn't even get registered at town hall. I have since had the event duly noted in the county records. I was born. And I was a child in that gully with the cats and the pigs and a mother who was perpetually some kind of catatonic."

"I don't see how that can be."

"Neither do I. You said you saw her?"

"Yes."

"The public school in Ada, Texas, taught me I could learn to read and write and do sums faster than anyone else. It also taught me I was garbage nevertheless, trash, something to be stepped on every day and thrown back into the gully every night.

"So one hot day I jumped a truck, and found myself in Dallas.

"Mister, you know nothin' about livin' in the street, unless you've done it."

Flynn said nothing.

"You eat out of the garbage pails behind restaurants. You sleep in abandoned lots and abandoned buildings. You get attached to a certain pile of rubble, where you've slept a few nights, and you bring things to it, little things you find around the streets, old magazines, paperback books, a ball, a broken kite, a broken Garrison belt. Then the people who live in that area come to know you're there and pretty soon the men and the boys come after you and they chase you away, throwing stones at you."

Flynn ran his eyes over the thousands of small, flaring fires along the shore.

"There were other men and boys, too," Udine continued. "They wouldn't throw stones. They'd stare at you in the street, and follow you around corners, and into alleys. I learned I was an attractive boy. I still couldn't live anywhere, actually live anywhere, or at least I didn't. But I could get clean clothes and eat in the front of sandwich shops instead of the back and, sometimes, some of the johns were interested in seeing I took a bath." Udine chuckled: "Literally."

Flynn said, "You became a prostitute."

"Sure."

"With women, or just—"

"Women aren't interested in boys that young. I was ten, twelve years old. I was with women later, of course."

"You were a whore."

"That's the word."

"You called your mother a whore."

"My mother was a whore."

"You were a whore."

"Yeah, but I couldn't get pregnant. I was a boy whore who went to the library."

"You mean in all this time, no one—not one cop, minister—no one took a good look at you, realized what you were doing, and tried to take you off the streets?"

"No one. Not once. Cops were to be avoided. Who knew from ministers and churches? I didn't. There was one librarian, a Miss Willikens, of Dallas Central Library, who was good to me. I brought her a list of words I didn't understand from books I'd read. She showed me how to use a dictionary. She talked to me about books and helped me to find good books to read. She was real good to me. Can you imagine a kid livin' the way I was, reading the *Penrod* books and gettin' a big kick out of them? *Peck's Bad Boy?* Everybody else read those books thinking what little rascals those kids were. I read them dreamin' of what their homes might be like. Of course, I never told Miss Willikens about how I lived. I suspect I made up some fancy story, right from the books she was giving me to read. I wanted her to think well of me.

"Then a drunken john left a camera with me by mistake, and that gave me an idea. I teamed up with another kid. We'd alternate. I'd do a trick and he'd take pictures; he'd do a trick and I'd take pictures. It was never hard getting into the pockets of these guys. They might protect their wallets, however they could, but usually they'd have an envelope in their coats, something, with their names and addresses on it."

"You went into the blackmail business."

"We did real well at it, too. Made real money. It came to an end, of course. Texans are real slow to anger, but once they decide they've had enough, they let you know in a real definite way. One week I got shot at. Twice.

"So I took a bus to New York.

"I was almost fifteen.

"More of the same there. Teamed up with other kids—boys, girls. But it was always my camera.

"By the time I was seventeen, eighteen, I had a fortune, a good suit, and had read everything I could lay hands on.

"I had a dream: to take over a company. I suppose I got the idea from all the books I had read. And it wasn't my idea to take over a candy store. I had read you could take over a small corporation for not much more money than you needed to buy a farm. I studied up on it some more. I studied everything. Even ran myself through a couple of business courses.

"When I was nineteen, I discovered the Udine Corporation."

"You mean it already existed?"

"It meant United Dynamics Industries of the North East. The stock was loosely held and worth only a few coins a share. I began buying it up. I changed my name. I got a job as a shipping clerk in the company. My name being George Udine caused some consternation at first, but everybody came to believe it was a coincidence.

"By my twenty-first birthday, I owned thirty-two percent of the stock, called a meeting of the directors, and had myself, the shipping clerk, elected to the board. Most of the rest of the stock in the company then just sort of fell into my hands."

"I don't believe that's possible."

"Oh, it was possible. I had spent almost two years in that company. You might say I knew the people well."

"You mean to say you had no resistance from the officers of the company, the board of directors?"

"None to speak of. I had photographs, you see . . . if not of them, then of their wives, their sons, their daughters. It's always been an operating principle of mine: in every family there's at least one damned fool; more, if you look hard enough."

Flynn said, "This is one of those questions I'm sorry I asked."

Dawn gleamed dully through the cloud of smoke caught in the valley of the lake.

George Udine emerged: a little man with quick brown eyes sitting on the stern thwart of the rowboat.

He was smudged gray from smoke and ashes.

Udine said, "My methods never changed much through the years. Buy cheap and sell dear: another one of your money clichés. I was almost always able to add an element to negotiations that caused other people to sell cheap and buy dear."

"Photographs."

"Photographs. Tapes, later, when there were tapes. Stolen financial records. Sometimes just good guesswork could turn a man purple. I bought companies for their real estate and real estate for what could be dug out from under it or built on top of it. Hotels, an airline, an instruments business—"

"The Udine Corporation."

"And that's how George Lewis became George Udine. I am very much a man of my time."

The fires along the shore had faded in the early-morning light.

Flynn locked his oars and began to pull for shore.

George Udine said, "Very much a man of my time."

Flynn said, "Seems to me you believed very much in money."

"I said it's a convenient medium of exchange. A kid like me had nothing to exchange for it except my body."

"And the blackmail? What do you have to say about the blackmail?"

"They used me. I used them back."

Flynn shook his head. "When I first talked to you, you called your mother a whore. You're a whore. You talked about your mother feeding garbage to the pigs. Yet you call money garbage and say you feed it to the people who work for you, whom you call pigs. Yet your mother is called crazy, and people all over the world say you're brilliant."

Udine said nothing.

Flynn ran the nose of the rowboat into the shore. Very little of the dock was left.

Softly, Udine said, "It all depends upon what people believe."

A helicopter was flying low over the eastern ridge of the valley.

Flynn stepped ashore, into several centimeters of ash.

Udine, moving stiffly, was getting out of the boat.

Every step Flynn took set up a flurry of ash. He

looked around. The steel parts of the dock were still recognizable; the foundation, a few beams, a section of the roof of the Shack; all around the shore of the lake there continued to be spirals of smoke.

Udine stood near Flynn, not looking at him.

Flynn said, "I suspect I have just seen a vision of your eternity."

Udine smiled.

He pointed at the helicopter. "They've come to see if I'm still alive. 'Fraid I have to disappoint them. You want a lift?"

Flynn said: "I'll walk."

The next night, Flynn arrived at the station where he had bought gas three days earlier. Twice on the long walk over Cleary Mountain he had found high, rocky places where he could lie down and rest awhile.

At first the old gas-station attendant did not recognize him. Flynn was covered with soot. Finally, the old man said, "Oh, yeah, you're the guy goin' up Cleary's Mountain to see old George. I was wonderin' what happened to you. You must have wanted to see old George real bad—but did you have to burn up the whole mountain to do it?"

24

Between airplanes in San Francisco, Flynn telephoned the Fraimans in Ada, Texas.

Marge Fraiman answered the phone. "Surely is nice of you to call, Mister Flynn."

He coughed. "Just wanted to know how everything is in Ada."

"You never saw such a mess. This place looks like it's been abandoned thirty years already. I didn't know a place could run down so quick. But—there's nothin' more we can do."

"How's your husband doin'?"

"Oh, he's doin' fine. We worked somethin' out with the Lord. Fact, it's a good thing you called today. If you'd have called tomorrow, you'd have missed us. We've been in touch with Sandy's old Bible college, you know, in Alabama? Well, we didn't know what else to do with all this money, 'cept give it to them, for the Lord's work. And they've offered Sandy a job there. Teachin'. Isn't that nice?"

"Very nice," coughed Flynn.

"Leavin' tomorrow, first thing. We're takin' that old Mrs. Lewis—remember the lady people 'round here called the pig woman—anyway, we're takin' her with us to our new life at the Bible college. Sandy's out packin' up the piggory now."

"Packing the piggory?" Flynn wondered how one packed a piggory. He decided he'd never know.

"Well, we can't leave the poor thing here, can we? She hasn't anyone else to look out for her."

"No," Flynn said slowly. "She hasn't."

"It's right nice of you to call, Mister Flynn."

"Delighted to hear everything's looking up for you," said Flynn. "All the best."

25

"Where are you, Frank?" N.N. Zero's voice sounded almost vexed.

"Hawaii."

"Should I ask you why?"

"Wanted to go for a swim. Besides, I need to be fed into Solensk, U.S.S.R."

John Roy Priddy inhaled, exhaled, inhaled, while Flynn waited.

N.N. Zero said, "Things are that bad?"

"Yes. I can only deal with the leads I have. I've pretty well discounted the eccentric-billionaire theory."

"You've talked with George Udine?"

"Yes."

"Any good my asking you why it took you four whole days to do that?"

"He was having a cookout," Flynn said.

"What?"

"There was a fire in his backyard that got out of hand."

"Did you find out all about him?"

"More than I'd ever care to know."

"What makes you decide he's not our Santa Claus?"

"George Lewis Udine is capable of anything, for fair reason or foul. But he couldn't remember the name of East Frampton, Massachusetts. He's been there, but the name means nothing to him." Flynn coughed.

"I don't think it's wise of you to go into Russia, Frank."

"Ach, sure, I promise you I'll carry it off with my usual beguiling charm."

"Why do you need to go?"

"One of the world's top ten counterfeiters, an American, has taken up residence there."

"I agree that's odd. But is it worth risking you?"

"I think so," Flynn said, coughing. "When suddenly great quantities of apparently good American money are plopped on unsuspecting citizens in three different places in the U.S."

"Four."

"Four now, is it?"

"Ten days ago, many, if not all, brokers on the Chicago Stock Exchange received little packages with you-guess-what inside."

"One hundred thousand American dollars cash money."

"Right on. And guess what happened as a result?"

"All the issues traded on the Chicago Stock Exchange acted erratically."

"You win the grand prize. The brokers threw this money into the exchange as only they know how, on margin, on options, every kind of crazy scheme. The whole exchange went wild. Shares of some companies hit the roof; others collapsed. Needless to say, the Chicago Exchange is now closed."

"It still sounds to me like someone is experimenting."

"Your conclusions, Francis, frighten us far more than have your solutions, to date."

"I'm sorry, sir," Flynn coughed. "I expect I'll find a frightening solution for you too, if you accept my best consolation."

"Why are you coughing so much?"

"Too much smoke."

"I've told you to give up that pipe."

"Right you are, sir, I'm sure."

"Are you making any sense out of this at all, Frank?"

"No, sir. Not one damned particle of sense. When I discovered Ada, Texas, had produced a billionaire who had also been to East Frampton Harbor, Massachusetts, my hopes fairly soared. But they ended in ashes, you might say."

"How do you feel? I mean, how do you really feel, besides the cough?"

"Oh, fine. As saintly as a lawyer who hasn't skewered a client in hours."

"Really, I'd rather send someone else into Russia, Frank."

"Ducey Webb?"

"Who's Ducey Webb?"

"That's what I'd like to know."

"Let's get together and think this thing through again. Money gets dumped on people, we can't find the source of the money; the people, the places have nothing in common; we can't find a common result—"

"I want to leave for Russia immediately, sir."

"Why?"

"People have been speaking to me about their ideas, things they believe in, everything from the devil walking the earth to the idea that you'll win at the crap tables if your son was just killed in an automobile accident, to the idea that the world is unraveling because of two sentences someone snuck into an ambassador's speech eighteen years ago. Religious ideas, psychological ideas, political ideas, economic ideas. I'd like to find the right idea behind this. Somebody believes something. . . ."

"Frank, I have about as much hope of ever understanding you as I have of becoming a basketball player. Mind running that by me again?"

"Communism is just an idea, isn't it? An economic idea?"

John Roy Priddy breathed in and out and in again. "Yeah. That's where I thought you'd end up."

"I haven't ended up there yet, sir. Fact, I hold out about as much hope for this Russia trip as I do for the hope you'll be a basketball player. It's something I have to check out."

"Call back in two hours. We'll have your marching instructions for you."

"Thank you. Will I get to talk to Ginger the Robot again?"

"No," said N.N. Zero. "He's out for repairs."

His twelve-year-old daughter Jenny answered the phone.

"Who is this?" she inquired politely at the sound of his cough.

"Francis Xavier Flynn," coughed her father.

"Who?"

"The man who comes by on the odd occasion to tune the instruments."

"Are you calling about the roof again?"

"Roof? What's wrong with the roof?"

"How many times do we have to tell you we will not, absolutely not, hire your company to fix our roof, no matter how badly it needs it, no matter how many times you call. My mother has told you, my brother has told you—"

"Jenny, darling, I'm calling long distance."

"Guess what?"

"If I have to guess anything again today," Flynn coughed, "my eyes will pop onto the floor."

"Randy gets to play the solo piece with the school orchestra, Saturday night. Todd's being very nice about it."

"A victory for each of them," Flynn said. "And what's your news, wee collection of fluff?"

"I got a seventy-eight in English."

"Is that percent?"

"Yes."

"Is that good?"

"I wouldn't say so, would you?"

"I'd be reserved in my praise."

"You should see all the horrible gook they make us read."

"I'm sure I have. Listen." Flynn coughed. "The other day I met a man who started out with nothin' at all in the world, a deprived youth, he was, more deprived you never heard, and he took to readin' and he read everything he could lay hands on, he said."

"And he turned out well?"

"No. He turned out to be a complete rat. One of the worst villains I've met to date, outside my own house."

"Just goes to show you."

"It does indeed. As Martin D'Arcy once said: It's not what's read that counts, it's who does the readin'. Well, that's not precisely what he said, mind you, but I don't think the man would mind my improvin' his line for him."

"Next English test I'll strive for eighty percent."

"Listen, be informed I'll be out of town a few days longer, and so inform your mother, and please ask her to inform the Boston Police Department I'm not recoverin' at all well from whatever ails me."

"Will you be home Saturday night for the concert?"

"I doubt it. But I'll be hummin' the Handel right along with you, wherever I am, and probably at a better pace than if I were at home."

"Well, I told you we don't want the roof fixed. One

just can't afford to hire labor, these days, what with inflation and all."

Flynn coughed. "You've got the lines just right. Hold the importuners at bay."

"Da, you're smoking too much."

"Ach," Flynn said. "I hardly smoke at all."

26

"TAAAOOO!" Flynn yelled. "ERK! YOW! UGH!"

He fell forward in the dark and struck his chin on the ground. Line was falling on him. His knees and back felt broken.

On the two-hour ride in the back of the helicopter from the British aircraft carrier Flynn had sat cross-legged on the floor, hands over his ears, glad he had eaten nothing. The noise caused searing pain in his ears. The vibration was sickening.

When the pilot waved at him, Flynn had stood up and clicked his parachute line to the overhead. The door opened. It was just before dawn.

The pilot gestured with his thumb.

Flynn closed his eyes and jumped out into the dark. Not his life, but his wife and five children passed before his eyes.

Now, from the ground, he looked up at the pilot.

The helicopter was only three meters from the ground!

"Ta," said Flynn.

The pilot slid open his window.

"Sorry, guvnor. Guess I brought you in a little lower than you was expectin'."

"Yow," said Flynn, on his back, knees up, wind from the rotor blades shooting sand into his eyes. He wondered how he could disengage himself from the parachute line without the force of G.

"Jumped with your eyes closed, did you?" the pilot shouted. "Bad habit, that."

The pilot waved cheerily. "See you tomorrow."

Suddenly Flynn's line began to move with the speed of a snake.

The pilot was taking off and Flynn was still connected to the helicopter.

"Hey!" yelled Flynn, as he was stood up by the line pulling taut. "Hey, up there!" he yelled as his feet came off the ground. "Hey, you!" he yelled as he found himself rising back into the sky.

Gravity or some kind hand broke his connection with the helicopter and again Flynn fell to the ground. The opening parachute fluttered down to cover him.

"Oof," said Flynn. "Ohhh."

Again he rolled onto his back.

He flailed the parachute away from his face.

A man in an overcoat and a wide-brimmed hat was standing over him.

"13?" the man asked quietly.

Flynn said, "How did you ever find me?"

"I heard you." The man pointed to some trees. "From over there."

"Not," Flynn said, "my most surreptitious penetration into a nation not precisely expectin' me."

"I'm N.N. 2842."

"Proud to know you," Flynn said from the ground. "Would you mind helpin' me remove my shroud?"

N.N. 2842 had expressed great uncertainty regarding the wisdom of Flynn's order that he park the three-wheeled car on the main street of Solensk so they could then set off on foot in search of breakfast and general information.

Solensk is a town, its buildings and its streets built of round gray stones. It is a small town, on a hillside on an island west of mainland U.S.S.R. in the Sea of Okhotsk. It is a small town, far from the capital, but it is still Russian.

N.N. 13 outranked N.N. 2842 by precisely 2,829 other N.N. male and female operatives at large in the world, plus, Flynn guessed, probably the robot Ginger as well, as soon as it was returned from the fixit shop.

So 2842, his eye sockets walled with concern, parked the little car facing downward on the hillside, its one front wheel against the curb.

"Sure," said Flynn, extricating himself from the car, "if we have to start somewhere we might as well start with something warm for breakfast. That's always the wise thing."

All the way into Solensk snow had been blowing across their path, from west to east. None had accumulated on the ground.

"Tell me." Flynn stood on the sidewalk, watching the horizontal snowstorm. "Doesn't even the snow settle here?"

A middle-aged woman passing Flynn on the cobblestoned sidewalk looked sharply at him.

2842, face horrified, dashed from his side of the car to Flynn.

"You're speaking English," he whispered in the wind. "Loudly."

"What's that? Well, of course I am. I don't speak Russian, you see. And I'm sure a dose of the old A-E-I-O-U will do them no harm at all. Now, where did you say breakfast is?"

"I don't know. I'm not from Solensk. I've never been here before in my life."

"Hell of a tour guide you are." Flynn started down the street. "Don't even know where breakfast is."

* * *

"Well, sure, isn't it a lovely day for doin' nothin' at all?" Flynn stretched his feet toward the potbellied stove.

They had found a restaurant down a few stone steps in the basement of a stone building with stone walls and a stone floor. The place was as warm as a sleeping puppy's belly. Flynn had removed his coat.

"There's something undemocratic about wearing a coat," he commented to the pale 2842, expecting to be chided for appearing in Solensk in clothes that may have been European or American but certainly not Russian. 2842 said nothing. He grew more pale.

Flynn had breakfasted on warm potato soup, black bread, sausage, potato patties, and five cups of steaming tea. Several times he tried to make conversation, in English, with 2842, but each attempt was greeted with silence and a nervous glance at a big bear of a man in a blue uniform sitting against one wall with *Pravda* and a cup of tea. The man had no insignia on his uniform but Flynn supposed he was the town cop. He did have a full walrus mustache.

"Blustery day like this, it's grand havin' a good cup of tea or five." (2842 had had only one cup of tea.) "Never been in Solensk before, eh?" 2842 said nothing. By now the cop had looked at Flynn several times. "Haven't missed much, I think. Good soup and bread and tea you can get almost anywhere in Russia. My, I've been in some dismal places lately, haven't I just? And it seems to me the wind's been blowin' in every one of them."

The cop stood up. He folded his newspaper under his arm. He came over to Flynn's table, and said something.

"Didn't quite catch that," Flynn answered the large man.

The man repeated himself.

Beads of perspiration were on 2842's upper lip.

"What's he sayin'?" Flynn asked.

2842 blurted in English, "He wants to see your papers."

"Ach, that. Tell him I haven't any."

2842 said, "You haven't any papers?"

"Well, sure," said Flynn. "My Massachusetts driver's license. My United States Social Security card. You can show him my wee badge as an inspector in the Boston Police Department." Flynn reached in his pocket. "That might impress him some."

He handed his badge to the cop, who looked at it right side up, upside down, and sideways.

2842 said, "You haven't even got a passport? A Russian visa?"

"In my other trousers," said Flynn. "I came away in rather a hurry."

The cop handed Flynn's badge back to him and said something.

2842 said, "He wants to know what you're doing here."

"Ach," said Flynn. "Tell him I'm a spy."

2842 stared at Flynn a long moment before speaking in Russian with the cop.

2842 looked down at the tabletop. "He says you can't be a spy," he said. "You don't speak Russian."

Flynn smiled. "Tell him I'm not a Russian spy."

Apparently 2842 did so.

The cop laughed and shook hands with Flynn.

"He sees," Flynn said, "I'm perfectly harmless. That I am. Invite him to take a cup of tea with us."

The cop dragged a third chair to the table.

"Tell him," Flynn said, "that as a spy I couldn't help noticin' that he didn't pay the proprietor for his mornin' tea break. Assure him that that universally is the policeman's custom."

The large cop laughed and shook hands with Flynn again.

While they had tea Flynn and the cop talked of the weather, which is to say the wind and the snow. Flynn admitted the ground that morning had been hard enough with frost to make burying his parachute difficult. The cop laughed.

"Ask him if he plays chess," Flynn said.

At the question, the cop became excited, stood up, called the proprietor.

"I think he's ordering up a chess set," said 2842, who still wasn't even slightly relaxed.

"No, no," said Flynn. "Tell him we can play later, if there's time. First we have to find and talk to—if we can—the great American counterfeiter, Cecil Hill. But don't tell him Hill's a counterfeiter. No use spoilin' the man's reputation where he's chosen to live."

The cop was reseated. He and 2842 spoke for some minutes. To Flynn the cop appeared listening, understanding, cooperative, gracious. Toward the end of the conversation an edge came into his voice and his face colored.

2842 said to Flynn, "He says the American, Cecil Hill, works at the large printing plant on the east side of town. He says he is very well regarded, as a printer."

"That's true," said Flynn. "Will you ask our man in blue what it is the printing plant prints?"

In a moment, 2842 answered, "Textbooks. Schoolbooks for all Russia."

"Not money?" Flynn asked.

The cop laughed when he heard the question.

2842 said, "The policeman says it is not a far walk to the printing plant and he'd be happy to accompany us to make sure we find the American Cecil Hill."

"Very obligin' of him," Flynn said. "But, tell me. I thought I noticed a little anger in the man, a moment ago, when he was speaking of the printing plant."

"That's because his nephew runs the place," 2842 said. "He doesn't like his nephew."

"Then neither do I," said Flynn. "Neither do I."

27

In fact, Flynn did not like the nephew, who was a skinny man in wire-rimmed glasses who moved too fast, spoke too fast, and generally demonstrated the impatience of a rooster upon first discovering why he had been put in the henhouse.

Flynn did not like the printing plant, either. Built of an ancient stone with red-brick wings, it was cold, damp, and dark. Walking through the plant to the administrator's office, he saw that the workers were sunken-chested and blue-nosed.

Red-faced from the beginning, Solensk's cop yelled everything he had to say at the nephew-administrator, apparently having to beat down the man's bureaucratic arrogance to get him to fulfill a simple request.

Finally, after a long moment of silence during which Flynn understood Cecil Hill had been sent for, a short, aproned, heavily sweatered, ink-stained man in his fifties entered carrying a single sheet of galley. He looked sullenly at Flynn, particularly his clothes. He spoke in Russian to the plant administrator, who shrugged indifferently.

"You're Cecil Hill?" Flynn asked.

"You're Irish?" Hill asked.

"Yes," Flynn said. "American."

"You're a cop?"

"When I'm at home."

"How the hell did you get here?"

"Helicopter."

"If you have any idea you're taking me back with you, to stand a mock trial in an American court and be put in prison for the rest of my life, you can forget it. Russia does not waste workers' talents."

"Unless they're intellectual workers or otherwise disagreeable," Flynn said softly.

"I'm much too valuable to these people, to the people of Russia, as a printer."

"I understand that," Flynn said.

"Then what do you want?"

"I know you're a good printer," Flynn said. "In fact, you're considered one of the world's top ten counterfeiters." Hill smiled. "Tell me, Mister Hill: do they actually have you living in a dacha? Your address is Dacha 11."

"It's no dacha."

"More like a cold-water room?"

"I had a dacha."

"At first?"

"Yes."

"And you're obliged to share your cold-water room with other people . . . ?"

"They're friends."

"I trust they're very good friends."

Flynn handed Cecil Hill the three American bills without saying anything about them.

Cecil Hill took them to the window and examined them.

"The twenty-dollar bill is a fake," he said. "A good one—good enough to fool some people—but it's a fake."

"And the fifty- and the one-hundred-dollar bills are not?"

"I don't think so. I'm pretty·sure they're not. To be absolutely certain, I'd have to use a microscope and some chemicals." He held the one-hundred-dollar bill up to the window light. "But it looks like somebody's already done that."

He handed the bills back to Flynn.

Flynn said, "Not your work?"

"What?"

"You didn't manufacture this money?"

"No."

"Mister Hill, in all the time you've been in Russia —especially when they had you ensconced in your dacha, stuffing you with vodka and caviar—did you design, or make, or in any way formulate plans for the manufacturing of United States currency?"

"No." Cecil Hill laughed. "An American flatfoot comes all the way over here on what you think is a counterfeit case? Wow."

"What we 'think is a counterfeit case'?" Flynn repeated.

"United States currency must be in some kind of trouble."

Flynn thought for a moment: . . . *think is a counterfeit case . . . United States currency must be in some kind of trouble. . . .*

"I think your phrasing has been helpful to me, Mister Hill."

"Delighted, I'm sure."

"I'm puzzled, nevertheless," Flynn said, "by one of the world's top ten counterfeiters living in one of the world's most unpleasant resorts?"

"I'm at home here, mister."

"But your peers are 'at home' on the French Riviera, in Paris, New York, California. . . . One is at home in federal prison in Marion, Illinois, of course."

"I like it here."

"But a man who has . . . let's say, the knack for making money you have—"

"What of it?"

"—to live under a Communist regime, which does not encourage the use of currency among its citizens . . . puzzles me."

"That's the point, mister. If I believed in money as a real thing I wouldn't have made the fake stuff, would I?"

"There's that word *believe* again. 'Believe in money.' I believe Satan walked the earth. My son was just killed, therefore I believe it is time I win a fortune gambling."

2842, still not an entirely relaxed man, was watching Flynn, listening to him closely.

"In the Western world, mister—your world—money is be-all end-all. Money! Just little bits of paper anybody can reproduce."

"Not anybody," said Flynn.

"Anybody."

"Anybody with certain skills, talents . . ."

"Anybody!" insisted Cecil Hill. "People run their whole lives, cradle to grave, centered on something totally unreal."

"Some do."

"All do."

"A good many do."

"All!" insisted Cecil Hill.

"You're saying money is phony anyway. . . ."

"Of course. Fake. All money is fake. An illusion."

"Excrement," Flynn said. "Garbage."

"No. Both excrement and garbage have some use. Money is totally fake. All money is fake."

"Ah, the darlin' mind of the criminal," said Flynn. "Endlessly fascinatin'. No mind believes more in justice than the criminal mind. All money is fake, *ergo* makin' more of it is no crime at all."

"Communism does not encourage a belief in money," Cecil Hill said. "A belief I didn't have anyway. I am quite comfortable here."

The man's socks were so thick he couldn't lace his shoes.

"I'll not be disturbin' your comfort much more," Flynn said. "But you did say how valuable you are to the Russian people. Just a matter of academic interest: if you're not grinding out the old buck for them, what is it you do that makes yourself so valuable to the people of Russia? If you don't mind my askin' . . ."

Cecil Hill hesitated a moment, then picked up the galley sheet he had brought into the room with him and put on the administrator's desk. He handed it to Flynn.

The light being bad in the room (except directly over the administrator's desk), Flynn took the galley to the window. It was in English. While the administrator sat at his desk, 2842 and Solensk's cop stood by the door. Cecil Hill stood close enough to the administrator's electric heater to turn the rest of the room colder. Flynn read:

THE BROTHERS' WAR, UNITED STATES OF AMERICA, 1861–1865, also known as THE AMERICAN CIVIL WAR and THE WAR BETWEEN THE STATES. In which the expansionist industrial Northern states provoked war with the agricultural Southern states. HISTORIC RESULTS: the South's black laborers lost their cradle-to-grave social and economic security provided by the South's plantation-slave system and became wage-earning slaves, without social and economic security, to the North's industrial system. Although granted paper "citizenship," the economic value of black laborers fell considerably, and fell again in the 1880s and 1890s when American Northern industrial capitalists discovered an even cheaper form of labor: refugees from the decaying imperialistic European systems (Karl Marx) lured to America by promises of land availability. Only enough land went to the immigrants (and that only to immigrants who had some capital; *grub-*

stake in the American idiom, i.e., enough money to buy food and other living necessities while land was being developed) to make the "promise" real. No land, no part of the economy went to blacks, as they were the conquests of THE BROTHERS' WAR.

Outside the window the snow was swirling furiously. Still, none seemed to be accumulating on the ground.

Flynn cursed his compulsion to understand comprehensively. Life is so simple, seen in black and white. In black and white and with a song on the lips. He'd had his chance at universal, eternal truth, twice, and found it boring. We live between the keys, between the chords, between the black and white. He'd lived between the borders. There is nothing more painful than a wide youth.

Flynn turned to Cecil Hill. "History in depth, is it? Is that what you're writing?"

"I don't write it. I only print it."

Flynn handed him back the galley. "Your mother would be proud of you."

28

"**W**ell, I'll be a monkey's psychiatrist," Flynn said.

He climbed the restaurant stairs to the sidewalk. It was still snowing but still no snow had accumulated.

It was two-thirty in the morning.

"I suppose this is what they call a nice night in Solensk."

2842 and citizens of Solensk, including the cop, were leaving the restaurant with him, arms around each other, slapping backs, saying goodnight. Having had nothing better to do, Flynn had returned to the restaurant with the cop after seeing Cecil Hill at the printing plant. He had been playing chess ever since. Other citizens of Solensk had come in to watch them play. Even Cecil Hill had appeared during some part of the evening and silently watched awhile. Although Flynn had kept himself to potato soup, cucumber soup, Russian onion soup, black bread, and tea, substantial quantities of vodka had gone down other throats, especially that of 2842, who had had a long and nervous day. Toward midnight he had begun chirping, in English, "I'm a spy, I'm a spy!" before falling asleep. During the afternoon and evening Flynn had become fond of the citizens of Solensk, especially the restaurant's large woman proprietor-cook, who apparently refused to believe anyone who could consume as much soup as Flynn did not speak Russian; the jolly bear of a cop, whose mood shifted manic-depressively depending upon the success of his chess moves; and a man who had entered the restaurant sometime during the early evening, sat in a corner, and played the clarinet beautifully.

"Well," Flynn said, stuffing 2842 into the three-wheeled car and waving good-bye to his friends, "this is not a bad old place at all."

Flynn drove. Beside him, chin on chest, 2842 slept.

It took Flynn more than an hour of driving around to find the right place to wait for the helicopter. That morning he had taken a casual fix on two distinctive peaks against the dark sky so he could find the place again in the dark, without 2842, if he needed to. He needed to. 2842 was dead to the world. To make absolutely certain he was in the right place, Flynn left the car and, after much searching in the dark, found the place he'd buried his parachute.

Then he sat in the cold car again. 2842 slept beside him. The wind whipped around them, snow blowing all sides.

All afternoon and evening, playing chess, Flynn had had the growing feeling that he knew something, was pretty sure of something, had heard something or, over time, had heard some things that fitted together somehow into a logic. A logic true to itself, but based on an insane or, at least, incorrect axiom. Cecil Hill. George Udine. Paul Sankey. Jimmy Silverstein, the Las Vegas comic. Marge Fraiman. Something Elsbeth had said . . .

Flynn poked 2842.

"I'm a spy," 2842 said, "I'm a spy."

"Talk to me," said Flynn.

"Where are we?"

"Waiting for the chopper."

"How did we get here?"

"By the seat of my pants. Thank you."

"It's still dark."

"It is that."

"Why did you wake me up? I want to sleep. I'm a spy."

"I have to make sure you're well enough to drive yourself home after I leave you. If the local authorities see the chopper coming in this morning they might come to believe I was serious. It wouldn't do at all for them to find you sleeping peacefully next to the pasture where the helicopter landed and took off, would it?"

"Not at all." 2842 sat up in his seat.

"Where is your home, anyway?" Flynn asked.

"Finland. I'm Finnish."

"You're a long way from Finland. You'll never make it in this car."

"No. I've been stationed the last six years over on the coast. At the campus."

"The campus of what?"

2842 looked across at Flynn in the dark. "K. campus."

"Oh."

"I'm a . . . uh . . . I'm a spy."

"You're almost awake," Flynn said. "Sure, we'll have you drivin' a straight line in no time."

"I'm a janitor," 2842 said, "on K. campus."

"Is it difficult?"

"Not very dangerous. No, I have plenty of time . . . to do what I have to do. The faculty is fairly stable. Not too many people outside the faculty are brought in to lecture."

"I'm sure of that."

"The student population is not very large—about four hundred at any one time—and I have plenty of time to get into their files, get good pictures of them —I mean, the students—even get to know many of them personally, observe their special abilities and characteristics beyond what might appear in their files. It's not hard work."

"How do they route your material out of the country?"

2842 hesitated. "Would you believe through Hanoi?"

"That is odd."

"Things get pretty well garbled in Hanoi, I guess. So much traffic through there no one notices. Then back to Australia."

"So you have personal knowledge of all the graduates of K. campus for the last six years?"

"Yes. I could say that."

"That will make you very valuable to N.N."

"I don't know. I would think so. Mostly I think they forget about me. You guys forget about me. I've never met anyone as high-ranked as 13 before. This is the first assignment they've given me off-campus in four years."

"You're in a sensitive spot," said Flynn. "You shouldn't be risked."

"I guess this assignment is pretty important." It was a question.

Flynn said, "It's not a counterfeit case."

"I was wondering."

Light was just beginning to come into the sky. The helicopter was late.

"Are there any particularly remarkable recent graduates of K. campus?" Flynn asked.

"They're all remarkable. And they're getting more remarkable every year. Brighter. Younger. Healthier. More perfectly psychotic. Frightening."

"I guess. There is a natural genius for creating dissension."

"Nice little bullets, now mostly aimed at the Third World."

"Tell me about some of them."

"Last year's most remarkable graduate was a boy,

about five feet ten inches, one hundred and fifty pounds, brown hair—so perfectly average in appearance you literally wouldn't notice him if you found yourself in a telephone booth with him."

"What's his specialty?"

"Disguise. Especially without the use of any makeup or props. He can change into something—I mean, someone—else right in front of your eyes. He can become a woman. An old man. An old woman. A child. While you watch. And completely convince you. He does it with his mind. Empathically, I guess. He thinks himself into becoming an old woman, and he does. With makeup and prop clothes he's impossible to detect."

"Languages?"

"Seven. Perfect."

"What's his designation?"

"Ground lion."

"You mean, like lion hamburger?"

"Lion on the ground."

"Lyin' on the ground?"

"I think you understand. Sir."

"Just makin' sure you're awake. I look forward to meeting Mister Ground Lion."

"You probably have. And after you have, you won't know it. I promise you."

"What I'd like to see is that damned helicopter. There's such a thing as carryin' innocence too far."

"And a girl who graduated four years ago. Frightening. The only one ever to achieve perfect scores at everything: academics, physical training, personality. Brilliant. And gorgeous. Her you would notice across the Sahara Desert with the naked eye."

"Specialty?"

"Brilliance. Beauty. Craftiness. Uncanny ability to manipulate people. In eleven languages, each spoken perfectly. Demolition ability, of course. Also heavy knowledge of fashion, design, art, and literature."

"Sounds fascinatin'. Were you in love with her?"

"Does the sun come up in the morning?"

"A little too quickly, some mornings."

"To see her is to love her. To know about her is to have your spine frozen right up to and including your back teeth."

"I think you're being overcome by sobriety," Flynn said.

"I never drink that way. Sir."

"I'm sure you don't. Do you remember that young lady's designation?"

"Who?"

"The young lady at whom you were just castin' a bafflin' array of praise and damnation."

"Deuce-Ace."

"Don't get you."

"Deuce-Ace. You know, you throw dice. One shows one spot; the other, two."

"But why? Why that?"

"That's the way she looks. I mean, when you look at her. She has one brown eye and one blue eye."

Flynn said, "I see."

"Usually K. does not choose people that distinctive-looking to train. But, as I said, she's brilliant."

"I see," said Flynn. "And beautiful."

"There's a brilliant black man, orginally from Ghana—"

Flynn heard the helicopter.

"There's my taxi. And barely in time to get me back for breakfast."

They both got out of the car.

2842 asked, "13, how do you get away with this kind of thing?"

"What kind of thing?"

The helicopter was in the eastern sky as visible and as noisy as a flying elephant.

"Marching into a Russian town, jabbering English, making friends with the local policeman, saying you're a spy, getting him to escort you around?"

"Local police are always very helpful," Flynn said.

"If you give 'em half a chance. It's in their nature."

The helicopter was kicking up more wind.

"But, saying you're a spy, 13! You got me damned drunk."

"Sure," said Flynn, turning toward the helicopter, "there's nothin' to spyin' these days, it's gained that much social acceptance, it has."

29

The admiral's aide was waiting on the flight deck for Flynn.

"Good morning, Mister Flynn. Nice flight?"

"Your pilot's sense of humor needs repressin'," Flynn said. "Please ask the man not to practice stalls in his flyin' machine when I'm aboard, especially before breakfast."

"Right, sir."

"He also dropped me off yesterday in a way that did my dignity little good and my trousers less. My trousers are important. The blasted cur. Lucky it is I'm alive, in one piece, and was able to do what I set out to do."

"A line is being held open for you."

"A line of what?"

"Well, I mean, a communication channel. To the States. Someone, your superior, I think, is very eager to speak with you, sir."

"Probably that blasted robot again," said Flynn. "Wants to tell me he's discovered a new motor oil for the relief of rheumatism, no doubt."

"What?"

The aircraft carrier had nosed out of the wind and was gathering speed.

"If you'll come this way, sir?"

"I'll have my breakfast, first," Flynn said. "That's the first order of the day—any day. Then, if you don't mind my twisting your communication channel a bit northward for the moment, I need to speak to my wife."

"Your wife, sir? Before your superior?"

"I never said my wife isn't my superior," Flynn said.

"Oh, is this the man calling about the roof again?" Jenny said into the phone in Winthrop.

She knew she was never to ask her father where he was.

"How did the concert go Saturday?" Flynn asked.

"Da, this is Saturday."

"Oh, I see. Well, wish all and sundry luck. Remind them Handel was composed, and so should they be."

"Handel was a composer."

"He was a composed composer, right up until he died. Then he began to decompose. He never became a decomposer, however. A compressor, yes, but never a decomposer. Try that out on Winny and see if he doesn't choose to starve to death in Las Vegas. Is your mother among the walking and talking?"

"I'll get her. Home soon?"

"Very soon, I think."

In the radio room of the British aircraft carrier, Flynn was carefully steering his breakfast—kippered herring, toast, jam, and tea—around the mouthpiece of his headset.

"Frannie?"

"Good day, old thing."

"You all right?"

"Like a bull who's never heard of a picador."

"Frannie, Jenny said she told you the roof needs repair. It really does. You know, winter—"

"I'll be home in less time than it takes a pig to burp, I think. I need you to thimblize something for me."

Elizabeth listened.

"Last time I was home, the kids got talking about inflation at dinner."

"Yes."

"You said something that interests me. When there is too much money around, where does it come from?"

"The government."

"Always the government?"

"Of course."

"Thank you, old thing."

"Is that all?"

"How much more can you get into a thimble?"

Flynn drained his tea mug and signaled the radio operator he was ready to talk to N.N. Guided by sound dials only (he was not wearing earphones), the operator switched Flynn to Frequency Red.

"13," Flynn said.

"That you, Frank?"

"It's yourself, is it?" It was N.N. Zero—John Roy Priddy. "Sorry to keep you waiting. Thought it would just be the gingery robot questionin' my expense sheet."

"You in one piece?"

"Hale and hearty, thank you."

"How was Russia?"

"I found this place—you might say a little, out-of-the-way place—that serves this fantastic soup. Three or four varieties of potato soup, of course, but each one of them excellent, a nice cucumber soup, and, frankly, sir, the best Russian onion soup I've ever had in my life. I would have brought you back some, especially some of the onion, but I was afraid it wouldn't survive the trip, you see, what with all the swoopin' up and down in the helicopter."

"Thanks for the thought. What else did you do in Russia?"

"Learned my manners at chess, I did. Brought back one or two perfectly rotten, devious gambits to try on old Cocky. That will surprise him well enough. Not that I lost all my games, mind you. There was a moment there, albeit short, that I was the disputed chess champion of Solensk."

"You found your counterfeiter, Cecil Hill?"

"I did."

"And . . . ?"

"This is not a counterfeit case. United States currency is in trouble."

"You learned nothing."

"I had a good think."

"Cecil Hill is not manufacturing United States currency for the U.S.S.R.?"

"He is not. He is coining history."

"Well, history is moving damned fast on this one, Frank."

"Oh?"

"There have been two more incidents of people being assaulted with money."

"Oh."

"One was an insurance company in Utah. Apparently everyone who works for the insurance company found an envelope on his or her desk Monday morning with one hundred thousand dollars cash in it. Usual results."

"Silent whoopees followed by instant devastation?"

"Thursday, literally thousands of envelopes, one hundred thousand dollars cash in each, were found in Denver, Colorado. Not even delivered to people. Just left in the streets. On buses. Lunch counters. In cars that had been left open."

"And the grand total is?"

"Incalculable.'

"Ginger the Robot can't count that high, even if he takes off his shoes?"

"The point is that now it's out in the open. The Denver largesse was so loose, so uncontrolled, everyone in town knew about it. The *Denver Post* ran a very good story about it this morning. The wire services have picked it up."

"That is the point."

"What's the point?"

"Rising expectations."

"What do you mean?"

"I mean I think I better talk to the President of the United States."

"Serious?"

"Yes."

"Right now?"

"Yes, please."

N.N. Zero paused for a moment. "Hang on, Frank."

"Thank you."

In the radio room of the British aircraft carrier, Francis Xavier Flynn, N.N. 13, poured himself a fresh mug of tea and waited. The tea was as hot and strong as he needed it.

Halfway down the mug of tea, Flynn heard N.N. Zero say, "Okay, Frank. I'm listening."

"Hello," Flynn said.

"What the hell are you guys doing?" asked the President of the United States. "United Press International is running this story out of Denver. Associated Press is running a follow about some similar incident in Utah I never heard of. Some damn-fool, disgruntled, retired Pentagon colonel is taping an interview at CBS."

Flynn said, "Hello, Mister President. This is Francis Xavier Flynn. How are you this day?"

"Hello, Mister Flynn. My favorite assassin."

"How are you sleeping, sir?"

"Fine, thank you."

N.N. Zero said, "Frank, you don't have to begin every conversation at the beginning."

The President said, "Do we have an emergency?"

"First, a question, sir," said Flynn, "I've been burnin' to ask you."

"Shoot."

"Sir?"

"Go ahead."

"A woman by the name of Ducey Webb . . ."

"Who?"

"Ducey Webb. Did you send her out to work with me?"

"No."

"You have never written a letter, in your own hand, concerning a woman named Ducey Webb?"

"I haven't written a personal letter since the California primary, Mister Flynn."

"I thought not."

"Not, I mean, in my own handwriting."

"Of course not."

"Did someone say I did? Did you see such a letter?"

"It's inconsequential now, sir."

"The money, Mister Flynn. That's a consequential matter."

"It's not a money matter, Mister President. It's a currency matter. As I understand it."

N.N. Zero said, "Frank . . ."

"Mister President, I think you have an emergency."

"How big an emergency?"

"Pretty big. Tell me, Mister President, how quickly can the United States shift currencies?"

"Shift it to what? What are you talking about?"

"Shift the current form of currency to some other form of United States currency."

"You mean, scrap greenbacks?"

"Scrap greenbacks. Yes."

"I know we can do it."

"You can?"

"Yes. We've had masses of blue currency, all denominations, including paper coins, stashed away for years."

"Where?"

"Warehouses. All over the country. All over the world."

"How long would it take you to prepare this blue money—may I call 'em bluebacks?—for general circulation?"

"That I don't remember. How much time do we have?"

"I don't know. Maybe a matter of hours. My daughter just told me we are coming into the weekend. . . ."

"My God, Mister Flynn. Do you know what you're saying?"

"Not really, sir. But I think it's worth the saying."

"What the hell are you saying?"

"I think, sir, you had better be prepared to shift currencies within a matter of hours. By the time the banks open Monday morning."

"Golly," said the President of the United States. "Dammit, I said, 'Golly.' As if the American dollar hasn't been under attack enough in recent years."

"Exactly, sir."

"Who's doing this to us?"

"You are, sir. No personal insult intended. I use the word you in the general, plural sense."

"Mister Flynn, your boss tells me you're on a British aircraft carrier somewhere?"

"Yes."

"Someone please make an arrangement to fly you here to Washington immediately."

N.N. Zero said, "I will."

"Come straight to the Oval Office."

Flynn said nothing.

N.N. Zero said, "He will."

The President said, "Mister Flynn, you're not saying we should actually put bluebacks into circulation?"

"I'm saying I think you better be all-the-way prepared to, sir. Plus I think you ought to consider every other option you have."

"I guess it's time we fell to a heavy dollar anyway."

"Exactly."

"People have been talking to me about it."

"I'm sure they have, sir."

"I guess I haven't been listening. Is this what it's all about?"

"I'm reasonably certain of it, sir."

N.N. Zero said, "What is what all about?"

The President said, "Devaluation. Damned devaluation."

Flynn said, "If you don't know why someone is doin' something, you have to look for the results of his doin' it."

N.N. Zero said, "Has someone been experimenting with dropping these packages of money all over the country?"

"No," Flynn said. "Someone has been warning the United States Government."

"And we haven't been listening," the President of the United States said. "Typical."

"Frankly, Mister President," said Flynn, "the signal hasn't been all that easy to pick up."

The President said, "Let me get this straight. Mister Flynn, you know the source of the money?"

"Almost perfectly certain, sir."

"And it is limitless?"

"Virtually."

"Come here immediately."

"Yes, sir."

N.N. Zero said, "I really hate to break in, but, Frank, what are you talking about?"

The President said, "The United States is about to be glutted with money. I mean, currency."

"More glutted," Flynn said. "More glutted."

"Mister Flynn, answer me the obvious question," the President said. "Is there any way to prevent this? To prevent what you think is about to happen?"

"I don't think so, sir. I would like to try, but I don't think so. This plot has been hatching a long time. It's pretty well thought out, if not perfectly thought out.

The fact that money was just thrown around in Denver, helter-skelter, gaining publicity, raising expectations, I think means the final switch is about to be thrown."

"The damned press has already announced this money that showed up in Denver is real money—not counterfeit," the President said.

"But, Frank," N.N. Zero said, "as long as the final switch hasn't been thrown, are you sure we can't prevent it?"

"We don't know the delivery system to be used," Flynn said. "Or systems. We can be sure no one's going to be tiptoeing around in the dark, dropping envelopes on people's doorsteps. That technique was just being used to warn us of what might happen. Or will happen. Or was happening, in its own way."

"Maybe the President understands you, Frank," N.N. Zero said, "but I've known you longer, and I don't understand you at all."

"Sir, I'm sayin' there's every good reason to believe the United States is about to be glutted with its own currency. I don't know precisely how it's going to happen. I think it's too late to stop it. We can't prevent its happening, but we can prevent the effect of its happening. If you understand me . . ."

"But if you know who is behind this . . . ?"

"If I may paraphrase my wife Elsbeth, sir: the most momentous events in history are apt to be caused by a little schnook with a grievance. . . ."

The President said, "Anything else, Mister Flynn?"

"Well, she also makes a darlin' soup, Elsbeth does. . . ."

30

As soon as the British Navy jet fighter landed at Andrews Air Force Base a dark blue Lincoln Continental sedan with District of Columbia license plates pulled up alongside it.

The dark-suited man who got out of the front passenger seat did not offer to shake hands.

"Mister Flynn? Name's Craig, White House aide. Have a nice flight?"

"Got some sleep."

"Orders are to take you to the White House immediately, sir."

"We're not going to the White House immediately, sir," Flynn said.

The man had opened the back door of the car.

"Sir?"

"We're going to Georgetown first."

"Sir? But, sir!"

A ten-dollar bill was fluttering in the air between them. They watched it fall to the ground.

Flynn looked up.

There were three or four more bills falling from the sky.

Near a hangar, a mechanic stooped, picked up a bill, looked at it, looked up, and shouted to his friends inside.

"Too late," said Flynn. "Here it comes. But I'm goin' to Georgetown anyway."

Craig picked up the ten-dollar bill and looked at it. Flynn knocked it from his hands.

Craig looked at him as if admonished, and then at the bill on the ground.

"What's the matter?" Craig asked. "Is it fake?"

"No," said Flynn. "It's real. That's what's so devastatin' about it."

The driver and the White House aide in the front seat, Flynn in the back, they drove into Georgetown an hour before dark.

Georgetown was bedlam.

Cash money was falling from the sky.

"Keep moving," Flynn ordered.

People were all over the street, some on their hands and knees, scooping up money, others running among the abandoned cars, jumping up and snatching money out of the air. In one corner, two men, each with fistfuls of money, were beating each other bloody. Shopping bags had been dropped in the street. One young woman, carrying a baby, stood on a curb, sobbing. They passed a policeman, carrying his hat upside down, full of money. An old woman was stuffing money down the front of her dress.

"Keep moving!" Flynn ordered.

People were jumping at the slow-moving car, grabbing money off the hood before it slipped to the ground. Through the windshield their faces were blind with greed.

The driver stopped the car, looked back at Flynn with wild eyes, put the gearshift in Park, and jumped out. He ran up the street, scooping up bills as he went, grabbing them from the air. He bumped into an old lady, hard, knocked her to the ground, stepped over her, and kept on running.

"Ah, well," muttered Flynn. "Prices being as they are . . ."

The aide remained where he was.

Flynn got out of the back seat and looked up.

Three airplanes were circling slowly in the sky, small pieces of paper— United States currency— streaming from them. There was no wind. Cash was falling on the city like confetti.

"Santa's reindeer," muttered Flynn. "A jolly old soul is he! And I thought he might be up to usin' the post office!"

Behind him, the window of a department store crashed. In the window, a man ran among the manikins, grabbing cashmere sweaters off them.

Flynn got into the driver's seat and put the car back into gear. He had to use the wipers to clear the windshield of five-, ten-, and twenty-dollar bills.

31

"I was hoping you'd show up, Flynn."

The front door of Paul Sankey's house had been left open, light spilling through it into the alley.

Standing in the living room–workroom door, Flynn said to Paul Sankey, "I should have listened to you."

Sankey was burning papers in the fireplace. The economics graphs were still on the wall.

"You did listen. You just didn't hear any more than I wanted to tell you."

He rose from the hearth and dusted his hands against each other.

"Oh, I heard, all right," Flynn said. "I think I even heard you confess. Or rationalize. Or whatever. You said all the right words. I just didn't put them together right. My mind wasn't prepared yet for such a monstrous idea."

Sankey dropped into the room's one upholstered chair.

Flynn moved farther into the room.

"You told me your Special Section had set up new systems to conduct the flow of money—of currency. That means a system for the Federal Reserve Bank's manufacturing new money. And a system for destroying old, worn-out money. Is that it?"

Sankey nodded.

"But you haven't been destroying the old, worn-out money, have you?"

"No."

"You've been stashing it away somewhere. Billions and billions of dollars."

"Billions."

"For years and years?"

"A few years."

"How did you get away with it all this time?"

"Anyone setting up any new system has the advantage," Sankey said. "You can build holes into the system no one sees. Others see what's there. Only the original designer sees what's not there."

"So instead of burning up the old currency in recent years, what have you been burning? I know for a fact the ashes from the Federal Reserve's incinerator are chemically analyzed."

Sankey laughed. "Newspapers. Slightly damp newspapers treated with the same chemicals, plus one rectifying chemical—again of my own design. I produced perfectly convincing ashes. Control saw the right amount of currency go into the top of the incinerator, and the right ashes come out the bottom. Need I point out the obvious to you, Flynn? That the incinerator had a false bottom?"

"Fascinatin'," said Flynn. "There's nothin' more dangerous than a frustrated man who's clever."

Sankey said, "I wanted you to know about it, Flynn, in case you and I didn't have this chance to chat. Frankly, I was delighted when you showed up at the Federal Reserve. It threw me off for a moment, because I didn't know exactly how far you'd gotten on this—what you doubtless call—'case.'"

"You've had a long-standin' belief in the deviousness of my mind," Flynn said. "Pity it hasn't been warranted."

"When I discovered you were only checking the validity of some bills, I had to laugh. At you, Flynn. At you. Here I was about to set the world on its edge and you came around like a rubber-hose flatfoot. After talking with you, at the Fed, I knew I was running free for the home stretch. You were too far behind me to catch up."

"You glommed my natural stupidity."

"You're not so stupid, Flynn. You're here."

Flynn said, "Not as early as I might have been."

"Then I had the desire, the compulsion, if you will, to fill you in as much as I could on my thinking. Without threatening implementation of my plan, of course."

"Thus the late-night lecture in economics. World Economics According to Paul Sankey."

"A nice piece of irony. Eighteen years ago you fed a couple of sentences into our ambassador's speech at The Hague."

"You're wrong about that, too, by the way."

"And eighteen years later—just as I'm about to rectify an historic error—you showed up. The same Flynn. The chicken comes home to roost. Nothing I wanted more than to have you witness the devastation you had caused. You or your people."

"And those two wee sentences surreptitiously inserted into the ambassador's speech at The Hague eighteen years ago—I know the ambassador quickly fled into retirement—but did they also ruin you professionally?"

"Of course. At that time there was no reason why I shouldn't have made ambassador myself, and by the age of forty. Anything irregular happens in a governmental career and one is shelved. Don't you know that, Flynn?"

"I've heard."

"It took me a long, long time to work back up—even to a Federal Reserve department head."

"You weren't the best choice for that job, either," Flynn said. "All in all."

"I think I was."

"You also think you're a great economist."

"I am. The greatest. I am the only man in the world who has understood, consistently, what has been happening to the American dollar, and thus to the whole world's economy."

"What you are," said Flynn, "is the economist willing to destroy the economy to make your own economic predictions come true."

From his chair, Paul Sankey's eyes ran along the graphs pinned to his wall.

"You're no economist, Flynn."

"No. I'm not. But I am a man with more experience with prophets, seers, oracles, and other damned fools than I'd care to admit. God save us all from people who act upon their idea of the truth!"

Sankey said, simply, "The Free World's economy could not be based permanently on the American dollar."

"And you set out to prove it, yes?"

"It was being proven. In the natural flow of events. No one listened to me. I was a clerk in the Fed. Right? I didn't have to prove it. Time was doing that. What I did is to reveal the truth. Now everyone will realize the world was headed in the wrong direction economically—had been for years and years. I've stopped the world from going farther in that direction."

"I suspect your cure is worse than our cold," said Flynn.

"Sometimes it is. Sometimes it has to be."

"Are you dropping cash money all over this country at the same moment by the same method?"

Sankey nodded. "No way you can stop it, Flynn. Human greed is being satiated coast to coast. There have been planes dropping currency over the nation's sixty largest cities the last two hours. Billions and billions of dollars. Used dollars, but real dollars."

"How did you get so many pilots to aid you in this horrible assault upon our well-being?"

"Money."

"I don't believe that."

"Money and a lie. They were paid in advance. Oh, they didn't know they were going to drop currency. They were given bags—which I designed and had manufactured—that would remain sealed until after they left the plane and hit the wind."

"What did you tell the pilots was in the bags?"

"Political pamphlets." Sankey smiled. "In a way, it was no lie at all."

Flynn said, "Do you know you're insane?"

"I know the world's insane."

"Same difference." Flynn took his pipe and tobacco pouch from his pocket. "Your wife and daughters were killed near National Airport by a three-axled army truck speedin' to deliver twelve dozen fresh flowers to a cocktail party at the Pentagon. Have I got it right?"

"That," said Sankey, "is only one incident of government waste. Excessive government spending, you might say, for less than desirable results."

Across the room, filling his pipe, staring at Sankey, Flynn said, "I'm sorry for you, man. But you have tried to create one hell of a mess."

"Is that all, Flynn?" Sankey stuck his right hand between the upholstered seat cushion and the chair arm. "Is there anything else you want to say?"

"Yes," Flynn said. "I think you've failed."

Curiosity in Sankey's eyes was only momentary.

He nodded agreeably.

Smiling, he drew a revolver out of the chair, placed the muzzle against his temple, and squeezed the trigger.

32

"You beat me, Flynn. You got here first."

Flynn was leaning over Paul Sankey.

"He's as dead as a greenback." Flynn straightened up and turned around, putting his hands in the pockets of his coat.

Ducey Webb, hands in the deep pockets of her overcoat, was standing just this side of the living room –workroom door. Behind her, the front door of Sankey's house was still open.

"What good did it do to kill him?"

"He did that himself," said Flynn. "A very self-directed man, he was. A poor little schnook with a grievance, as a friend of mine would say."

"Oh. Coming up the alley, I heard the shot . . ."

She did not appear disturbed by the sight of the suicide in the chair.

"Ducey Webb," Flynn said.

She looked blankly at him.

"You're a gorgeous lass."

"Thank you."

"Beguilin'."

Her expression did not change.

"Bright enough too, I hear. Tops in your class. Brilliance. Beauty. Craftiness. Uncanny ability to manipulate people. In eleven languages, each spoken perfectly. Demolition ability, of course. Also heavy knowledge of fashion, design, art, and literature. At least, that's what I've heard."

Her expression still did not change.

"The faculty at K. campus are proud of you, lass. Tell me, were you American originally?"

"You've heard a lot, Flynn."

"I get around, I do. Somewhat. Deuce-Ace. Ducey Webb. The devil herself, spinnin' her web. Lookin' forward to a limited career, I suspect, due to two outstanding physical distinctions: rare beauty, and eyes that don't match, however entrancin' each of them is on its own."

"You never accepted my act, did you?"

"I did not. Your disappearin' off the road for half an hour that day you were following me in Texas had to mean somethin', I still don't know what. Then, you must realize by now, gel, a note of introduction in the President's own hand was a bit much to believe, although providin' no signature was a nice, convincin' touch. A simple, 'Hallo, Mister Flynn, what-are-you-doin'-with-yourself-this-fine-day?' might have sufficed."

Her eyes were equally smoky.

"That's all right, lass. It was a young person's mistake. Using an atomic cannon to kill a gnat is the common expression for it."

"Thanks for the lesson in Introductory Skullduggery," she said.

"That's all right, lass. You're only four years away from the old campus. There are lessons yet to be learned. But how did you match up all this currency floatin' through the air with the peaceful man reclinin' behind me with parts of his head missin'?"

"I knew you had visited Paul Sankey before—here at his house. So I found out who he was. When the money began falling out of the sky all over the country this afternoon I knew there could be only one source of so much money."

"The Federal Reserve Bank itself."

"Yes."

" 'So much money,' " repeated Flynn. "So very much money. But, tell me, lassie: if you're so brilliant, why have you connected up with the K. bunch, I want to know? Are you that set against peace and prosperity?"

"You and I don't happen to believe the same things, Flynn."

"Ah, lassie: I don't believe anything at all. Well, I believe in breakfast and the occasional cup of tea."

"Bullshit."

"Instead of believin'," said Flynn, "I'm a great one for tryin' to understand."

"Then you should be able to understand me . . . and K."

"I understand," said Flynn. "A bit. But I don't accept. You know, most of the people in the world want to make their way forward slowly, through education, enjoyin' what health and peace and prosperity they can. Bombs goin' off all sides of them have a way of bein' distractin'. Certain things can be accomplished by war and violence, for sure. Even certain good things. But K. violates all sides of the world at once, to bang it into some shape thought desirable by only those few who run K."

"You have no idea who runs K."

"But I know your organization is as old as the hills, and, historically, it has devoted all its energies to diminishing the world and all the people in it as much as possible."

"It's really very simple, in concept," said Ducey Webb. "Hungry people are easier to govern."

"I know. Oh, Lord, I know. You might say K. has manifested itself to me more than once in my short years."

"I know all about that," said Ducey Webb.

"Do you?"

"I know all about you."

"Wish I could say the same."

"You know, Flynn, K. had no hand in this."

"In what?"

"In all this. The United States being flooded with its own currency."

"I know."

"We knew it was going on. I guess we knew about the incidents in East Frampton and Ada before you did."

"And you rushed right in to investigate?"

"We didn't understand it. Not at all."

"Neither did we," said Flynn. "As is clear."

"It looked so much like something we at K. might be doing. We've tried something like this before, in Israel, in Chile . . . K. figured the quickest way to find out what was going on was to get someone to cover you."

"You wanted to have a good look at it to see if it was something you might want to take credit for?"

Ducey Webb smiled. "We might yet."

"Do," said Flynn. "Be my guest."

"It seems to have worked out. The American dollar is ruined."

"Down, but not out," said Flynn.

"The capitalist system got so overblown it burst."

"Lots of people like it," said Flynn. "The words *free enterprise* still have a nice ring to 'em."

"You're overblown, too," she said.

"Without doubt. But was your education at K. campus good enough to answer me one small thing?"

"Try me."

"Eighteen years ago at The Hague the American Ambassador gave a speech. Someone slipped two sentences into that speech. Apparently the speech, and those two sentences in particular, set the tenor of the Free World's economy ever since. At least our silent friend, Paul Sankey, thought so. Do you know what those two sentences were?"

Ducey Webb said, " 'The European Common Market will never attain an economic force equal to that of the United States of America. It is in full cognizance of this that the United States of America assures European Common Market nations of the full support of the United States of America.' "

"You got it right the first time," Flynn said. "Those two sentences were planted by an agent of K?"

"Sure."

"Nice piece of work."

"I think so. Those sentences did more than anything else to put the Free World on the dollar standard. If nothing else, it caused the oil-producing nations to reject the concept of Special Drawing Rights and demand payment for oil in American dollars only."

Flynn looked at Paul Sankey in the chair, the front of his head shot away.

"As the supply of oil went down," Ducey Webb said, "the supply of dollars went up. In a way, I guess, what happened today—money all over the streets—was inevitable."

Flynn thought of Marge and Sandy Fraiman, Joe Barker, Helen and Parnell Spaulding, Gabriel and Alida Sims, Ronald and Barbara Ellyn, Milton and Jackie Schlanger, Cindy Lownsberry, Major William Calder, General Seiler, Colonel Perham, Colonel Seely, Major Rosenstone, Lieutenant DuPont, Adele Hughes, Hulett Weed—all the ruined lives and careers: *inevitable?*

"So K. can take credit for this anyway," said Flynn. "Every logical system must have its axiom, true or false."

"What?"

"Just rattlin' on," said Flynn. "Just rattlin' on."

With no change in facial expression, Ducey Webb drew a .45-caliber automatic from the pocket of her overcoat and aimed it at Flynn.

"There you go again, lass," chided Flynn. "Usin' an

atomic cannon to kill a gnat. That's a hell of a big gun for a wee slip of a girl."

"Chauvinist."

"Somehow I don't think that point is worth debatin' at this particular moment, I don't."

"My training says to kill you. You know who I am."

"On the other hand, lass, the door behind you is open."

"Why wouldn't I shoot you?"

"Well, it's a short life, at best. . . ."

Ducey Webb said, "Somehow I get the feeling I'm making a mistake."

"I have a riddle for you, lass. How can a man shoot himself in the head without a gun?"

Her eyes flickered around the room.

"Where is it?"

"In my pocket, pointed between your matchless eyes."

Deuce-Ace said, "Oh."

N.N. 13 said, "Oh."

"All right." She put the handgun back in her pocket. "There's not much you can do about money falling from the sky at this point anyway."

"Go tell K. the sky is falling. Make sure you people take credit for it."

Ducey Webb said, "This time it's a draw. Right?"

Flynn said, "Somethin' like that."

Keeping her eyes locked on Flynn's, Ducey Webb backed slowly out of the room and out of the house.

After she left, it took Flynn a moment to find Paul Sankey's gun. It had fallen to the floor the other side of his chair.

"No one believes a lie as well as a liar," Flynn muttered to himself. "Isn't that the truth?"

33

Sitting at his desk in the Oval Office, the President of the United States put down the telephone when Flynn entered. Through the windows behind him were the lights of Washington.

He stood up and shook hands with Flynn.

"It's a great pleasure, seeing you come through that door, Mister Flynn . . . instead of coming at me, gun in hand, through a wall!"

"Would you mind closing the drapes behind you, Mister President? It's a simple precaution, you know, doesn't cost a farthing. . . ."

"Oh, yes. Of course." The President pulled the drawstrings. "Funny no one has ever thought of that. Sit down, Mister Flynn, sit down. Did you ever see anything like this? Money falling from the sky—all over America." The President laughed. "And who says I don't keep my campaign promises?"

Flynn laughed with the President.

"Would you believe, Mister President, that drivin' over here just now I saw money lying in the streets? Nobody's even bothering to pick it up anymore."

"Too much of a good thing," smiled the President. "Coals to Newcastle; greenbacks to Washington." He sat down again at his desk. "I'm sure the street sweepers will have it cleared up before dawn."

"Will they?"

"Sure. The street sweepers of Washington, D.C., are more sophisticated than nine-tenths of the Congress. At least they know shit when they see it."

"You seem in a rollicking mood, Mister President."

"Why wouldn't I be? I wish all crises were as happily resolved as this can be. So the country went on a binge for the weekend. They're entitled. Now that I've got you here, tell me who, what is the source of all this money?"

"A poor little schnook with a grievance. A disgruntled clerk at the Federal Reserve. An economist willing to destroy the economy to make his own predictions some true. An insanely grief-stricken man whose wife and daughters were killed in a tragic accident a few years ago."

"All one in the same?"

"All one in the same."

"Has someone put him in a straitjacket?"

"He gave himself an inexpensive lobotomy," Flynn said. "With a handgun. A little more than an hour ago."

"Oh. I see."

"He was the man in charge of incinerating the used money at the Federal Reserve. He built a false bottom in the incinerator."

"Oh. I'm surprised no one ever thought of that before."

"It's not quite as simple as all that. All the devices set up to guarantee that the used money was being destroyed properly he also had to circumvent. I'd guess he'd been given too much of the new system to design himself."

"He must have been a clever person."

"Just got mixed up between his enemies and his friends," said Flynn. "I've known it to happen before."

"Is that the whole story?" asked the President. "Is that all there is to it?"

Flynn hesitated. "Yes." He would make his full report to N.N. Zero later. It was difficult enough, traditionally, getting presidents of the United States to grasp the concept of N.N. Getting them to understand K. would be impossible. "Yes, sir."

"Well, I consider it a great stroke of good luck."

"You do?"

"Indeed I do." The President was doodling on his desk pad. "I've been being told now for a long time, by my advisers, that we have to devaluate. In fact, the dollar is worth only ten or twenty cents now, and the whole world knows it. However, it's an admission we've been unwilling to make. This gives us the perfect excuse. We have an awful lot of dollars out there in the world beyond our borders."

"More than half a trillion dollars," said Flynn. "Whatever that means."

"Whatever that means," agreed the President. "So much it's really unthinkable. And the cheaper the dollar's been getting abroad, the cheaper oil has been getting for everybody else, and the more expensive it's been getting for us. This thing had to smash up sometime."

Inevitable.

"We have lots of options," said the President. "And, thanks to you, we've had the time to implement them. That thirty-six hours warning you gave us makes all the difference."

"Thank you, sir."

"Monday morning, everyone in this country takes whatever Old Dollars—greenbacks—to the banks and gets so many New Dollars—bluebacks—in exchange. We haven't figured out yet whether they get either one or two New Dollars for ten Old Dollars. The damage hasn't been completely assessed yet. Members of the Cabinet are about to come in and so advise me. Prices —prices of everything from gold to common stock to services and bread—will fall accordingly, within hours. Monday noon, for example, your wife will be able to buy a loaf of bread for a dollar and a half, old currency, or fifteen cents, new currency. Soon, as a Chinese philosopher might say, there will be no more Old Dollars—those which currently are out blowing around the streets—in circulation."

"I see," said Flynn.

"Now, you see, thanks to our crazy friend in the Federal Reserve Bank, everyone knows the dollar isn't worth anything."

"I'm beginning to think he wasn't so crazy."

"What was his name, anyway?"

"Paul Sankey."

"Thank ye, Paul Sankey. It was an insane thing to do, Mister Flynn. But it's an ill wind, et cetera."

"He said he was doing it only to reveal the truth."

"Or, another option is to do away with the cash-money, currency system altogether."

"Did I hear you?"

"Right. One of our banks in particular—actually, it's Citicorp—has been setting itself up for years to shift us completely to a credit system. No cash in circulation at all."

"No cash money?"

"None. Your income is paid directly into the bank. You have credit for whatever additional savings you have. You are given something like a credit card, identified by your Social Security number, which is also your income-tax identification number. You carry this around with you. For everything you have to pay—highway tolls, lunch, groceries, even a house—you simply present your card and things are charged up accordingly."

"And tell me," asked Flynn, "what does that leave you to give the odd beggar in the street?"

"It's not a bad idea," said the President. "For one thing, it would make the collection of taxes a great deal easier."

"We'd all like that," said Flynn. "Wouldn't we?"

"Another great thing about all this," said the President, doodling, "besides bankrupting organized crime, is that we jerk the magic carpet out from under all foreigners—particularly the oil-producing nations—who are holding American Old Dollars over our heads."

"Ah, yes," said Flynn.

"Accepting payment for oil in nothing but American dollars has bankrupted us, you might say. So they're going to get ten cents back on their dollars. Surprise, surprise! That will teach 'em for buying six out of every ten United States Treasury bills we've issued the last few years."

"I should think so. Indeed, yes."

"As of this moment, the Free World is off the dollar standard," said the President of the United States. "The world can use gold, spices, oil, toothpicks, S.D.R.'s, whatever, I don't care. But, as of this moment, the international foolishness about the dollar has stopped."

" 'Thank ye, Paul Sankey,' " repeated Flynn. "But, surely, Mister President, the inside of this cloud isn't solid silver, is it?"

"What do you mean?"

"I mean, it is a crisis, isn't it?"

"A manageable crisis, Mister Flynn. A manageable crisis. Under de Gaulle, the French devaluated sharply to a New Franc. France's economy has been much stronger ever since, as a result. Devaluation gives the American economy a whole new life."

In his mind, Flynn saw the scrub pine blowing down the empty main street of Ada, Texas. What had he been thinking then? What he was being told: *Satan walked the land. There had been an earthquake. Banks had extended too much credit to the ranchers. There was no oil under the land worth thinking about. . . .*

And he thought of the Las Vegas comic Jimmy Silverstein: . . . *here we all are in this big sandbox called Las Vegas, playing with money . . . because it isn't real anymore!*

. . . and of sitting through the night in a rowboat on a lake, surrounded by hell's fires, George Udine saying: *I make money because other people believe in it. I collect garbage because pigs want to eat it. . . .*

. . . and of Cecil Hill, a great counterfeiter, standing in the cold, dank room of a printing plant in Russia, saying: *Both excrement and garbage have some use. Money is totally fake. All money is fake. . . .*

Francis Xavier Flynn was sitting in the White House Office of the President of the United States.

"Somehow," said Flynn, "I'm surprised to be sitting here, at this moment. Are you trying to tell me, Mister President, that Paul Sankey didn't commit a crime at all? That he's some kind of a hero?"

"No. Not at all," said the President. "What he did was insane and criminal. All over the country, all over the world right now, people are huddled, frightened beyond belief. The world, as they know it, has collapsed. They know that the American dollar, as they've known it, believed in it, is worthless. They are in real pain. Terror. What's going to happen to them, to the world, without the unholy buck?"

Flynn said, "I know. But in the morning, you'll give them something new to believe in. Is that it?"

"Bluebacks. Credit cards. New Dollars, somehow. Be assured, Mister Flynn, the American economy is still incredibly powerful."

"I'll tell my wife."

"It's just little green pieces of paper that aren't worth much at the moment."

"Excrement. Garbage. Tissue paper."

"And I'm not waiting until morning." The President glanced at his watch. "I'm going on television in two hours."

Flynn said, "I thought that was a sparklin' new shirt you're wearin'."

"As soon as I know what all the answers are."

"Then I don't see what Paul Sankey did," said Flynn, "that fills you with such rollicking joy?"

"That's easy, Mister Flynn." Looking up from his doodle, the President grinned. "You tell me a little nut over at the Federal Reserve made the sky rain money, right?"

Flynn said nothing.

"So," said the President of the United States, "one, poor, unfortunate, insane employee at the Fed, acting alone, gets blamed for the immediate, worldwide currency crisis. The entire United States Government does not get blamed. As long as people continue to believe in us—whether we deserve it or not—we're home free."

Flynn stared at the President silently.

There was a rap on the office door behind Flynn. He heard the door open.

The President laughed. "Don't worry, Mister Flynn. This office isn't bugged."

From the office door, a voice asked, "Are you ready for us, Mister President?"

"Anytime," said the President.

He stood up to shake hands as members of the Cabinet, the secretaries of Treasury, State, Defense, etc., trooped into the Oval Office.

The President said to them, "Now let's see precisely what we're going to do about this problem."

The last person with whom he shook hands was Francis Xavier Flynn.

"Good night, Mister President."

On the pad in front of him the President had sketched a rural scene—a valley with a house, a barn, a pond, a few cows, a horse—a perfectly peaceful scene.

"Good night, Mister Flynn. Always nice doing business with you. Thanks for droppin' by."

About the Author

Gregory Mcdonald is the internationally successful author of the FLETCH and FLYNN mysteries. He is the only mystery writer to have won the prestigious MWA Edgar Allan Poe Award consecutively, for FLETCH (1975) and for CONFESS FLETCH (1977). Prior to devoting all his time to writing novels, Mr. Mcdonald spent seven years at *The Boston Globe* as Arts & Humanities Editor and as a critic and columnist. His other books are FLETCH'S FORTUNE, FLETCH AND THE WIDOW BRADLEY, WHO KILLED TOBY RINALDI? and FLYNN. THE BUCK PASSES FLYNN is the second book in the FLYNN series. Mr. Mcdonald lives in Concord, Massachusetts, with his wife, Susi, and their two sons.

Ed McBain's Classic

87th PRECINCT

Mysteries...

"The best of today's police stories...lively, inventive, and wholly satisfactory." *The New York Times*